SCORCHED HEARTS

EMILY HAYES

1

ELLE

The sudden uproar of sirens shook firefighter Elena Rodriguez awake from a shallow nap. Her body already knew where to run. Tense like steel armor, her muscles settled into the familiar routine of urgency – she slid down the pole to the ground level of the fire station, seeking out information from one of the captains.

"Pearl Avenue – school fire," Deputy Chief Ramirez yelled through the speakers.

. . .

The crew prepared two fire trucks to be dispatched. Elle settled into her usual driver's seat, a privilege which she'd earned. In her mind, she prepared for the worst. Even in a city like Phoenix Ridge, bustling with life and modern architecture, schools could be a real fire hazard. Their outdated heating systems and wooden structures often raised goosebumps on Elle's skin.

In a matter of seconds they were on the road, wailing sirens blazing above their heads, the life corridor stretching ahead. The citizens of this city could never catch a break from emergencies.

Upon reaching the school, a familiar mixture of relief and nauseating irritation rose. Ahead of their trucks lay a picture of a perfectly idle day, kids playing around and laughing on the school grounds, though some were already raising their heads to stare at the annoyed firefighting crew.

A group of alarmed teachers emerged out of the building, their hands nervously flying around in the air. A woman at the front of the group began hastily apologizing.

. . .

"Oh, God, I swear I had no idea how to turn the alarm off! Some first grader pressed it and before we knew it, your trucks were here."

The false alarm call went the way they all did, with a reminder to call the station immediately if there'd been a mistake, the principal's suggestion that maybe the firefighters could visit the school sometime to talk *some responsibility* into the kids, and Ramirez saying she would consider sending a bunch of young firefighters over one day.

Eventually, they all got back into the trucks and drove peacefully back to the station. Elle couldn't help but feel pure relief on the way. As frustrating as a false alarm was, she was always relieved when nobody died.

The rest of the shift passed uneventfully, unless one counted destroying Kaia Montgomery in endless rounds of cereal poker as an attention-worthy detail.

. . .

"Kaia, you have the worst hand I've ever seen," Johnson laughed, while sliding another row of cereal loops to her side of the table. Slightly melted, they kept sticking to her palms.

Haley Johnson had only recently joined the crew and kept surprising everyone with her out-of-pocket talents. Apparently, one of them was a penchant for poker.

"Wanna feel it?" Montgomery threatened with a fist.

"Don't get my hopes up. You're taken," Haley Johnson retorted and made the whole company laugh like thunder. Kaia only smirked, resigned, and licked her remaining loops from the table.

While driving home to the melody of her favorite Nirvana album, Elle's thoughts spun around her date the next day. She had finally asked the cute barmaid from a bar down her street for her number. She'd been frequenting it far more often than necessary in hopes of figuring out whether the charming woman might be single, and on top of that, interested in women.

Elle's charms had clearly worked, but then, it wasn't a surprise, really, and Mimi—that was her name—accepted the drinks invitation. Elle wondered for a while whether it might be a *faux pas* to invite a barmaid to a bar, but she'd always thought the classic first date locations were best. Mimi didn't seem to mind.

Having effortlessly parked her car, Elle stood next to it for a moment, contemplating a cigarette. The evening embraced her with a light, humid breeze, and she gave in. The lighter clicked deliciously, and her first drag in a few days tasted to Elle like heaven. Swaying gently, she stood contemplating until the neighbor's car parked right next to hers. She waved.

. . .

Mrs. Dumas got out of the car, clearly in a bad mood. She and Elle weren't on the best terms.

"I thought firefighters were supposed to be a good example to citizens." She loudly shut the door to her Mercedes.

Elle took a long drag, then said, exhaling smoke, said, "We're supposed to fight fires."

Mrs. Dumas scoffed, unfastening her sleeping son from the back.

"I live here with small children. Your smoking disturbs their health."

"No more than the pollution produced by your car... Besides, I'm four yards away from you. They'll be fine."

. . .

Mrs. Dumas was now leading the sleepy child up their excessively long steps, her eyes full of disdain.

"And to think my taxes are paying you for all--" she gestured vaguely at Elle's house, "—this! For just sitting around and once in a blue moon extinguishing something. Incredible."

Elle waited until the door closed behind them and laughed. God forbid people who work with their hands deserve a space in this neighborhood. Having finished her cigarette, she cast the butt on Mrs. Dumas's yard and went inside.

Elle sat in her car, impatiently checking her watch. Its leather strap was ill-fitted, either too tight or too loose, and Elle, being too lazy to pierce a new hole in-between, simply wore it in a way that always fell down her wrist. After checking the time, she had to twist it back up again. Light rain hit the windshield in delicate splatters, clouds rumbled about the sky. She tried remembering whether she'd heard anything about an approaching storm, but nothing came to mind.

There were still ten minutes left until 6 p.m. Elle hated being early. She felt it made her look too eager. Her tall, toned silhouette suggested a stoic demeanor, and she was trying to lean more into that image, even as it slowly caused her burnout. With each new short-lived fling, she grew more appreciative of her effortless first love, back when she didn't have to curate her behavior, back when she could just *be*.

She spotted Mimi nearing the bar's entrance, walking on foot with no umbrella. Elle shut the car door and followed.

"You're all soaked." Elle leaned in to give her date a casual hug. She briefly stroked Mimi's back before taking her seat at the bar, her elbow resting against it like a man's.

. . .

"Well, nice to see you, too." Mimi fluttered her eyelashes. "I never noticed how tall you are."

"Oh, I like it when you swoon at me." Elle smirked, winking at the barman that they were ready to order.

Mimi laughed, sounding like little bells.

"Stop teasing." Sshe looked Elle up and down. "I've been waiting for you to ask me out for quite some time."

"What's your drink of choice, Mimi?" Elle switched the subject.

"Hmm... I'd say a Lavender Aviation. How about you?"

. . .

"That's a fun choice." Elle nodded. "I'll take plain old whiskey, then."

"Well, that doesn't come as a surprise to me. I remember every drink you've ever ordered, and most of them were whiskey."

"Oh, that sounds as if I have a problem. Sometimes I have fun with a Martini." Elle smiled. She knew she drank too much and smoked too often, but she figured a barmaid wouldn't care.

Their conversation flowed well, just like the drinks. Mimi's skin glistened beautifully in the bar's dim light, contrasted with her cream slip dress. Her voice grew husky and rich the more she drank, lavender liquid swirling in the glass held by her supple fingers.

"How do you get along with... male firefighters...?" Mimi's question came out slightly slurred.

. . .

"Are male firefighters what you want to be talking about now?" Elle laughed a little. "There aren't any in Phoenix Ridge. It's mostly all female."

Mimi furrowed her brows, confused. "Why, though?"

"You know what this city is like. Women have all the power. I don't know why, to show that we can do it on our own, fight prejudice, all that. And we get along great."

"Do you have lesbian firefighter orgies?" Mimi laughed.

"Very funny," Elle pulled her face closer, leaning in for a kiss. "Now let's shut your pretty little mouth, hmm?"

. . .

Doe-eyed, Mimi licked her lips and obediently leaned in.

Elle felt the same dread she'd felt on her previous dates. Mimi's mouth felt great against her own, and glancing at her legs, she could see her thighs trembling a little with anticipation. But whatever pleasure or excitement Elle felt, it was purely instinctual and not the deeper connection she'd been secretly craving.

Her hand began playing around with the hem of Mimi's dress.

"Let's get you to my car, how about that?" she asked, getting up to settle the bill.

Mimi nodded, dewy-eyed with alcohol and the premise of fun. She fixed her lipstick in a little compact mirror, then threw it back into her purse.

. . .

"Come on," Elle beckoned.

They left the place holding hands, stumbling a little on the steps outside.

"That's the car," Elle pointed towards her Audi, faithfully parked at the farther end of the parking lot.

"Oh, it's very nice." Mimi nodded. "I didn't know firefighters earned that much."

Elle looked silently at her, amused at how people always underestimated how much throwing oneself into fires and crumbling buildings paid. Elle worked every overtime shift going. And she always worked holidays, and they were double pay. She did all right for herself. She opened the door for Mimi, then walked around to sit behind the wheel.

. . .

"So, where do you live?"

"We're going...to my place?" Puzzled, Mimi looked back at her.

Elle gently stroked her thigh, causing Mimi to shiver.

"I hope you don't mind?" Elle much preferred away fixtures. That way she could leave when she was done.

The drive passed in relative silence, as it turned out Mimi lived very close by. Elle parked perfectly close to the curb, then unfastened Mimi's belt.

"Here we are. It's a nice building." She nodded.

Mimi smiled in response, waiting for Elle to get out. But Elle had promised herself something back in the bar. She wouldn't go through another meaningless night again, a kind of hedonism she wasn't sure even counted as hedonism, since it brought her no actual pleasure. These evenings with random women had become a painkiller she'd grown used to, and after a while, the habit had become ingrained in her even as the premise of relief had long ceased to deliver.

"Goodnight. It was pleasant to meet you, Mimi." She threw her another charming smile.

"What do you mean? Aren't you coming inside?" Mimi clutched her purse, confused. "Did I do something wrong?"

"No, no." Elle shook her head. "You're wonderful, trust me. I just don't think I'm up to it tonight. I don't want to wake up in the morning and be just another body who's passed through your bed." Mimi raised an eyebrow, so Elle quickly added, "Or you mine, for that matter. Or you mine."

. . .

"Okay." Mimi opened the car door. "But you were the one who asked for my number."

The she slammed the door. Elle's forehead met the steering wheel as her mind fought off waves of regret.

Nothing would be different this time, she kept repeating to herself. *Nothing at all.* She drove away from Mimi's house never to return again.

2

MAYA

"Sylvia?" No response. Dr. Maya Monroe's knocking grew louder. "Sylvia, please it's me!"

She dropped to the floor, exhausted. Her disheveled bag lay in the middle of the corridor, turned upside down in search of her keys to no avail. Her digital wrist watch displayed *02:34 a.m.* like a mischievous ghost, taunting Maya. She banged on the door again, and with every dull sound, she grew even more painfully aware of her trespass.

Miraculously, the door creaked open, and Sylvia's tangle of hair peered out.

"I don't want to be a bitch, but aren't you getting too old to be doing this?" She yawned, watching Maya scramble to collect her bag's contents.

"You know how it works at the hospital," Maya whispered, running to get inside the flat.

Sylvia locked the door and went into the kitchen. "I'm making tea. Do you want some?"

"You're an angel." Maya sighed. "I'm so sorry. Once I move out, you'll finally have some peace."

"Yeah." Sylvia's voice reached her through the sound of boiling water. "You'd think out of the two of us, I'd be the one asking to be let in at 3 a.m."

Maya giggled to herself, massaging her temples. The dull, pounding pain pulsed through her body. She dreamed of nothing more than a hot bath and clean bed sheets, but her bones felt stuck to the dining room chair.

"How are your finals going?" Maya asked, wanting to remedy her disastrous interruption.

"You know, you sound like my mother." Sylvia came in with two steaming cups of green tea.

She was a law student from Germany, almost ten years younger than Maya. At night, thrown out of deep sleep, Sylvia's accent would grow stronger, adding a foreign lilt to her words.

"Sorry." Maya took a sip of the tea, burning her tongue and hissing like a cat from pain.

They sat at the dining table in the light of the moon, amidst elongated shadows and blue hues. Maya finished her tea and got up to take the cups back to the kitchen. Her joints wildly protested in pain, making cracking sounds on the way.

"You move as if you're fifty." Sylvia yawned.

"Go back to sleep," Maya shouted from the kitchen. "I don't want you failing exams because of me."

"Whatever you say." Sylvia trotted-off to her bedroom.

Maya let her face completely relax, releasing all the built-up tension from the day. Her hands felt sore from multiple surgeries, even after two painkillers, and she knew the only remedy would be to rest. There was no time to do so, however, with the entire moving business. Her belongings lay around half-packed in the particular chaos of changing where one calls home.

She made her way to the bathroom, keeping the light as dim as possible to ease the stinging behind her eyelids. The bathroom was never as clean as she'd like it to be. For now, she convinced herself it was due to Sylvia's messy nature, but in no possible world could Maya herself keep her surroundings clean. On her free days, she wanted either rest or exhilaration unrelated to home or work.

At this point, she'd saved up so much by sharing a flat, that she could easily afford to hire someone to clean her house every day. But the concept made her feel strange. No, she was saving up to acquire real estate. Something her parents could never dream of but she'd finally achieve.

The bath melted her soreness away, and content, she quickly fell asleep.

"I think I found the perfect flat for you," Maya's real estate agent, Arthur, filled each word with the perfect mix of professionalism and joy they teach at business school. Or so she imagined.

"Send me over the pictures and everything, and we'll talk once I get to the city, all right?" Maya looked around her empty room. "I still have a lot to do regarding the move."

"No problem," Arthur chirped. "Good luck moving!"

For now, Maya was moving into an empty rental of her old, high-school friend. She didn't have much to transport, since she didn't own any furniture besides her silver-framed mirror, but she didn't have a large car, either, and Phoenix Ridge was located basically at the other side of the state.

"Need any help?" Sylvia popped her head into Maya's bedroom, chewing on a carrot.

"You mean *can I help you, so I can procrastinate studying*?" She flashed Sylvia a warm smile. "Sure, I'm not your mom. I need to carry the boxes in the corridor downstairs."

Sylvia eagerly followed her to the corridor and grabbed a box.

"For fuck's sake, what do you have in there?" she panted.

"Books. Have you ever seen medical textbooks?"

"Didn't you finish school like years ago?"

"Law and medicine have this in common—we never stop learning." Maya winked and descended the stairs with piled up carton boxes in her arms.

The day welcomed them with a clear sky and warm sun rays dancing along the road. The truck Maya had ordered was late, and the driver called to apologize for an hour and a half of delay, to which she could respond with nothing besides *no problem.*

"Do you want to go for a goodbye coffee?"

Maya suggested as they carried the last box to the lobby downstairs.

Sylvia nodded, and they headed toward the only cafe nearby, which served bitter coffee to exhausted adults and half-melted ice cream to crying children. Gossiping teenagers sat around slurping on banana smoothies, their straws getting stuck in their braces.

"I'll miss our once-in-a-month movie nights," Sylvia confessed, savoring her iced latte.

"Me ,too." Maya nodded. "We can do them online, though."

For a moment, she sat in silence. All her formative memories were contained within the city of Phoenix Ridge, and now she'd be moving back to it all.

"Why'd you leave in the first place?" Sylvia asked after a while. "Isn't Phoenix Ridge a bigger city?"

"Bigger doesn't always mean better." Maya sighed, "But in this case, yes. I didn't get the position I applied for there, but I got an offer from Forest Vale Hospital. After I settled in at Forest Vale, I was learning a lot working under Dr. Roman, I really saw no reason to go back. But now that the opportunity has arisen at Phoenix Ridge

Emergency Department, and with a much better salary...it was a no-brainer."

The other reason remained unsaid, emotions lying dormant for years lazily stirring in Maya's chest, preparing to wake up once she returned.

They enjoyed the nice shade formed by the alley trees, watching toddlers crawl around the lawn and parents chasing after them. Maya thought fondly of her time at Forest Vale, but she had no doubt she wouldn't look back. Part of her regretted not taking steps to move back to Phoenix Ridge earlier. The opportunity had come to her as a true blessing. Phoenix Ridge was home.

"Do you miss your parents?" Sylvia prompted.

"Hmm... I wouldn't say so." Maya smiled. "I think we work best when at a distance from each other. I like to call from time to time, but we have our problems," she concluded.

Sylvia nodded. "I get it. But also, it's a sad thing to say."

"Not necessarily. They have tensions between each other, and that can sometimes affect the kids, too. I'm really close with my brother, though," Maya remembered with fondness the adventures she and her older brother had gone through together. "I can't wait to see him."

The truck driver called, and they quickly ran back to the apartment. Packing went smoothly, the truck turned out to be more than big enough, and it was time for Maya to part with her life in Forest Vale. She hugged Sylvia tightly, promising to stay in touch even if she went back to Germany.

"I don't think I will, though." Sylvia laughed.

"Well, you never know when or where you might come back."

Maya got into the driver's seat of her own little Fiat and embarked on the journey home. As she drove through the serpent-like highways, she almost felt herself going back in time, unravelling her life and tracing the various paths stretching out like asphalt in the sun, melting and twisting together like a bunch of roads with destinations yet unclear.

"I want it." She sighed, standing in a gorgeously lit apartment hidden away in a quiet alley minutes away from the city center. "I really want it." There was a lovely view over the city and the forest to the south. She could even see the sea out of the big window in the bedroom.

Arthur, Maya's real estate agent, pressed his hands together. "Well, you can easily afford it. Your financial situation is strong, and you've already prequalified. Shall I prepare all the documents?"

Maya nodded, enchanted. This was real. She was about to buy an apartment entirely on her own, to furnish it on her own, and do whatever she'd like with it. Even the sun streaks seeping in through the windows took on a celebratory shape in her eyes.

Having taken the documents to read later, Maya headed straight toward the Main Phoenix Ridge Hospital. Blood pumped through her veins at an insane speed. This was the dream, the place where she'd wanted to work from the beginning.

The apartment and the hospital together seemed to her such a pinnacle of achievement that they almost overshadowed an icy sensation rising in her chest while passing certain corners of the city.

No time for that. She shook her head decisively. It was time for her to get to work.

3

ELLE

"Maybe you're a poker prodigy, but you sure aren't a *treasure chest* prodigy," Elle proudly exclaimed, extracting from Haley Johnson the two aces she'd been lacking to complete her set.

"Somehow *treasure chest* prodigy doesn't have the same ring to it." Johnson shrugged. Up to this point, she hadn't managed to collect a single *chest*.

Before the women knew it, the alarm rang its bestial tone around the station. Their playing cards fell to the floor as everyone got up in haste and one by one slid down the pole to the ground floor of the station. The ringing took on a nasty intensity, which meant it was serious.

In a choreographed manner, each took her equipment, then her place in the truck. Not a single second of time to waste. *Quick. Efficient. Highly Trained.*

"We are meeting the trucks from Station 20, Station 4, and Station 22. Building Fire."

Four trucks meant large fire. Elle took the driver's seat and waited for coordinates.

Captain Hunter coordinated their departure. Roaring sirens wailed above their heads as they made their way toward one of the oldest residential buildings in town.

"We knew it would happen eventually." O'Malley sighed.

. . .

No one knew how to respond, and Elle was too occupied with maneuvering the huge fire truck around the busy streets. Otherwise she'd tell O'Malley to shut it and get off her high horse. There were people there potentially burning alive. In the supposed safety of their homes. The chill running down her spine at the thought reminded her each time why she'd committed to this path.

They saw the rising black smoke from several miles away. It swelled and ballooned, tugged on by the gentle wind. The situation looked grim. When they got to the scene, Elle could see the residents gathered outside. There weren't many, thankfully. Due to the afternoon hour, most residents were probably still at work or commuting. What a view to come home to.

Captain Hunter was busy checking in with the concierge, while Captain Ramirez checked the building's state with her crew, doing a 360 and analyzing the structural damage the building had suffered.

. . .

"It's safe to say everyone is here," the concierge said, nodding. "The fire spread slowly at first, so we were able to double check most rooms. Some were more flammable and they practically exploded."

A car frantically parked right next to the fire trucks and a distressed man stormed out of it, looking around the gathering at the parking lot.

"My sons!" he shouted, tears streaming down his cheeks, "My mother! They're in the building!"

Hunter looked sharply toward the concierge. "You said everyone was here!" Then she shouted into her radio, "An ambulance urgently needed. Team 2, prepare to go in."

Then she hastily took the man aside. "Which part of the building? What floor?"

. . .

Elle immediately put on her mask and pulled on her fire hood and helmet, preparing to go together with O'Malley and Montgomery. They exchanged meaningful glances, mentally going through the worst case scenarios and their immediate solutions.

"Third floor, from our perspective to the left, room 34," the man recited, on the verge of passing out. "My little son called me. He's there with his brother and my mother."

"FLOOR THREE, WEST, ROOM 34," Hunter barked at them. "Team 2 on evacuation. Team 1 on water."

Two ambulances arrived at the parking lot and the paramedics hastily spilled out of them, setting up equipment and scanning the crowd.

"This man's about to pass out," Hunter

commanded them in passing, then went over to the fire truck to instruct Team 2.

Elle and O'Malley kept Montgomery in the middle as they moved into the building. The heat produced in Elle a familiar sensation. This was go time. This was what they trained for. Her muscles screamed, protesting each step farther into the blazing inferno.

"Staircase intact," she communicated via radio to Hunter.

"Ascend."

The old stone-carved stairs felt steady beneath their feet, carrying the weight of their gear. The first floor past them. Elle tapped Montgomery's shoulder. "Not so fast. We stay together." Kaia slowed down again, evenly in step with the other two. The terrifying sight of melting metal welcomed them on the second floor. Windows twisted into nightmare-like shapes and flames licked the walls like a pack of starved animals hunting for food, swarming insects devouring the building.

The three firefighters looked for the staircase, but a part of the wall had fallen, obscuring the path. Elle took out her axe and with a monstrous effort raised it to break through the wall. The other two carefully stepped back as she tore the piece of wood to shreds. They moved through, testing the floor's integrity as they went.

Third floor.

"Team 2 on the third floor," Elle barked into her radio.

"Got it, Elle. Go West."

The heat-resistant compass wavered a little before establishing the direction. To the right.

To the right. The sentence kept burning into the

inside of Elle's mind. It was impossible to see through the smoke. The only thing that mattered —go to the right, rescue, descend. At the moment, nothing existed for her besides these three tasks. Nothing would exist at all if she didn't focus all her strength on finding the three people and bringing them out.

"RODRIGUEZ, HERE! Flat 34." O'Malley waved them over to the door frame.

Elle and Kaia ran to assess the structure. Someone inside was faintly crying. They had to pull open the door, grab the victims, and get out. Elle could hear Team 1 fighting the fire. O'Malley used a hook to pull on the wavering metal, and it gave in after a few seconds. In the oven-hot shambles of the room, an elderly woman lay unconscious together with a small boy. Next to them, a barely awake boy cried, stuck to his wheelchair. Swiftly and efficiently, they dragged the woman down the stairs. Elle moved backward with her grip tight around the woman's chest. She felt nothing but pulsing pain in her muscles, ringing in her ears, and the determination to look ahead, look ahead, look ahead. O'Malley and Montgomery carried one child each and they lead her out. At least the stairs were clear of fire, and there was some visibility. It was a quick, efficient exit. Would the woman and the children survive? Elle desperately hoped so. this aspect of the job never got easier.

They reached the exit. Cold air outside embraced all three heroes, and the medics crowded about them, securing the victims on the stretchers, shouting to each other things Elle had no strength to decipher. Elle pulled her helmet and mask off and breathed the cool night air. Captain Hunter ran up to congratulate her and her two other teammates, but the words seemed to Elle out of sync with her mouth. They twisted and bent in strange ways around Elle's ears. Everyone seemed as if they were behind a thick glass barrier, dull and blurry, and when she opened her mouth to say something, her voice sounded removed from her body. Elle wasn't feeling right. She needed help.

. . .

Captain Hunter took hold of her just before she collapsed, "Rodriguez? Oh for Christ's sake, why are there only two ambulances around?"

She waved a paramedic over while taking Elle by her shoulders, removing her breathing apparatus, loosening her fire jacket and gently laying her down.

"Don't worry, they'll help you in a second." She nodded encouragingly. "You did a great job, saving those three. You guys were smooth and quick. It wasn't an easy task."

But the words only wobbled around Elle's mind in abstract shapes. Soon, a medic ran up to her carrying a spray bottle and some cloth. Her figure seemed very familiar, the way her hips moved in a hurry, the way she kneeled on the grass taking over supporting Elle's legs. As she got closer, the earthy scent of her body mixed with the same perfume she'd been using for decades raised goosebumps on Elle's skin. She tried focusing her vision more, but her doubt was useless—it was Dr. Maya Monroe kneeling right next to her, her straw-blond hair tied as neatly as it always had been.

"Breathe in deep, please." The voice sounded as cold as the compress that landed on Elle's forehead.

"You still haven't changed your perfume?" Elle tried laughing, but a wave of nausea overcame her.

Maya didn't react besides coldly unzipping Elle's jacket in one professional motion.

"Oh, you're undressing me now?"

"You have heat exhaustion, and we need to get out of your jacket so we can cool you down."

. . .

Maya was clearly not in the mood for a warm reunion, though Elle considered it might also be due to the circumstances. She looked toward the ambulances. One had already departed, and in another there seemed to be a commotion. The building was still being extinguished, but there was no risk of the fire spreading. She weakly wriggled out of the jacket.

"Raise your shirt."

Elle did just that, this time without any comments, though many crossed her mind. Immediately, she felt cool water sprinkled on her skin, causing shivers to ripple through her body. This made her feel better immediately, the fire of her skin finally dwindling down.

Maya handed her a bottle of cold water.

"Drink up. I'll stay with you until another ambulance arrives and a paramedic can actually take care of you if something happens."

. . .

Elle frowned.

"Aren't you a paramedic?"

"No, I'm a trauma surgeon. But they dispatched too few ambulances. I stabilized the boy. Now he's going to the hospital, look." She pointed toward the ambulance getting ready to leave. "But we can't leave you guys without an ambulance, so we'll wait until they come."

Maya truly hadn't changed much. Her light hair rested tightly bound, the color she'd once explained to Elle was *strawberry* blonde, but when Elle pointed out another blonde, Maya insisted that Maya's hair wasn't *strawberry* blonde but *sunflower blonde.* They laughed it off in the end.

The weight of memories nested somewhere at the bottom of Elle's chest.

. . .

"Why'd you come back?" Her voice came out much more meek than she would have liked, little vibrations of emotion on the string of her words.

Maya turned to look at Elle's face—an intense stare difficult to endure. Elle turned away, regretting the question.

"I don't think it's any of your business, Elena." She shrugged, collecting the equipment in one place.

Elle raised herself up on her elbows, feeling significantly better under the cloudy sky. Evening was approaching, and her skin breathed in the cold water from refreshing compresses. The firefighters were still in the middle of wrestling with the fire, and a few cars had pulled up at the parking lot, hopeless residents of the building who'd got back from work to see their home had been ruined. Some held little children in their arms, some came with teenagers, some had no one to turn to and watched their undoing alone.

. . .

"Where are you staying?" Elle was desperate for at least a small piece of banter, if not to rekindle Maya's affection, then perhaps at least to distract her from being unable to help any further. Heat exhaustion would keep her out of work for at least two days, and she'd have nothing to do. Work was her life.

Oh, and whiskey and women… The three beautiful W's. But she had given them up, hadn't she? Women, at least.

Probably a hangover had caused the heat exhaustion. She had to stop drinking on nights before she had work.

Maya let her hands fall in resignation.

"Elena, I don't want you to talk to me. We no longer have any kind of personal relationship. I'm here as a professional doctor to watch you in case you pass out. As soon as my colleagues arrive, I'm gone."

Elle's breathing got heavier. She'd thought that once they'd settle into their separate lives, they could be at ease with each other. That she could treat the woman she'd known inside and out as a friend, even if their paths had at some point diverged.

The woman she'd never forgotten.

"Am I supposed to pretend nothing between us has ever happened?" Elle brushed her hand against Maya's, but it was quickly shoved away.

"No, you're supposed to act according to what happened." Her voice trembled a little, but she quickly took control of it. "Take responsibility for your actions for once in your life, Elena. Your truly shitty actions. Remember them?"

. . .

Elle sighed. She needed a drink.

For fuck's sake.

The atmosphere between them grew irreversibly sour. Maya was as beautiful as ever, especially when she was pissed. The ambulance still hadn't arrived, and the other one was preparing to leave. Maya ran up to it to consult the plan, leaving Elle alone for a moment. O'Malley and Montgomery, having rested, were helping the crew extinguishing the fire, and the situation appeared to have deescalated quickly.

Elle's stomach swelled with another wave of nausea, rapidly paling her skin. She crawled over to the water bottle, gulping the cool liquid. The clear taste of it swam down her tongue, but the painful nausea exhausted her. Slowly, her eyelids grew heavy, and she plunged into a feverish sleep.

"You okay? Elena?"

. . .

Someone was touching her shoulders. When she opened her eyes, it was Maya again. She smiled, feeling stronger.

"So worried, how sweet." She tried sitting up to prevent falling asleep again.

"No, lie down."

Elle obediently followed Maya's cold command, so contrasting to her head-spinning heat of fire and abruptly met old love. After a moment, she tried again. "Could we cast aside what happened and be on normal terms? Maya, it's been so long…"

Hearing her own name leave Elle's mouth made Maya subtly flinch. Her arms grew tense, and in the dusking sun, Elle could see the shimmering drops of sweat create silver paths along her skin. Maya's presence did something to Elle that she hadn't experienced with any other woman, not before nor since. Her bones itched with want, the heat of their reunion beat in her heart with more intensity than the fire blazing next to them. And in the heart of that beating fire of her chest, something poisonous dripped. Melted. Elle began feeling the poisonous little pangs of guilt.

Maya turned to look at her, a prolonged, cool stare meant to hide her trembling heart. But Elle saw the corners of Maya's mouth twitch, and she knew everything she needed to know.

"You hurt me, Elena. You hurt and humiliated me. And after all this time, I'd hoped you'd grow up enough to see that your actions have consequences. You play with fire – you get burnt. Maybe you got that idea messed up after all these years running into burning buildings."

Elle swallowed spit louder than she'd intended to, and in a small voice said, "Very clever."

. . .

Maya wasn't finished. Now that she'd uncorked her hurt, Elle knew she would go all the way.

"I know no one's going to tell you this, but you're not untouchable. To have something real you need to make real sacrifices, put in real effort! This doesn't only apply to your job. Love is work. Becoming a decent human being is work. And all these girls, these girls who throw themselves all over you because of the way you look, because you're a hero—how's that working out for you?"

Elle kept quiet. She hadn't expected Maya to hit such a sensitive nerve for her. But Maya had always known her best. She shook her head. "You think I'm some kind of a playboy."

"Aren't you? I just think you take intimacy withoutsacrifice yourself, over and over again. And I can't imagine you've changed much. You use women and then discard them. You know the best part, Elena?" Her voice rose dangerously high.

. . .

Elle shook her head. She'd entirely forgotten about the dizzy spells or the nausea she'd felt. Her body lived whatever words Maya directed at her, absorbed every break in her voice, every twitch of her expression.

"Everyone I tried dating in Phoenix Ridge after you, they thought I was just another Elena Rodriguez cast off just like all the rest. That I was just a toy you'd gotten bored of. And you know," her voice broke, "I found it difficult to refute."

These words absolutely enraged Elle. Maya had been *different*. Maya was... She grabbed Maya's hand, and this time wasn't immediately pushed away.

"That's bullshit, and you know it. One drunken mistake doesn't change anything about the kind of deep connection we shared for years. I'm sorry, you know I am, but--"

. . .

"No, I don't know, Elena." Maya pulled her hand away and got up from the grass. "Frankly, I don't care. I moved away. I got over you. I'm back now, but I'd like for us to keep our interactions to a minimum."

She pointed to an approaching man. "My colleague will take care of you."

"I feel fine now." Elle grunted, hurt by Maya's words.

"Don't be a baby," Maya responded and was gone in a moment.

Elle's vision became blurry with tears. The male paramedic kneeled next to her, checking her temperature. The building stood almost entirely extinguished, its image now flooded by tears in Elle's eyes.

. . .

"How are you feeling, ma'am?"

"Who does she think I am?" Elle moaned, fed up with herself more than anyone else. "I fucked this up."

The young paramedic sat next to her, confused.

"I'm not delirious," she explained. "tThat doctor is my ex."

4

MAYA

The crowded surgery room began filling up with the scent of sweat, overshadowing even the usual synthetic smell of chemicals and surgical equipment. *Why is there such a crowd here?* Maya couldn't help the thought bouncing about her mind even in the middle of performing surgery.

She was having a hard time adjusting to the new work environment, especially after the recent dispatching mistake.

. . .

She remembered her encounter with Elle Rodriguez and sighed. A leopard never changes their spots. And sometimes, when someone had caused you enough hurt, you couldn't just forgive and forget.

However goddamned attractive Elle still was, dirty and distressed from the fire.

Either way, with the chest stabilization finished. Maya was desperate to get out of the OR and finally eat something. Her stomach rumbled without mercy. The sweat-filled rubber gloves landed gracelessly in the trashcan full of identical pairs, blood stained and disgusting.

On her way, Maya passed a nurse she'd made friends with. Both of them were new to Phoenix Ridge hospital, though Fleur came from abroad.

"Hi." Maya waved. "Up for lunch together?"

. . .

"Sure." Fleur smiled. "Cafeteria, or do you have your own?"

"You know I do," Maya laughed, and they headed for the lockers.

Another reason for her finding it difficult to socialize was that she suffered from celiac disease and could never eat anything from the hospital cafeteria where the majority of doctors and nurses found time to make conversation during their scarce breaks. Fortunately, Fleur also brought her own vegan lunches.

"How is it going?" Fleur asked, taking out her box of pasta from the staff microwave.

"Wanna know the truth?" Maya sighed. Her salmon didn't look particularly appetizing.

. . .

Fleur nodded, encouraging. She was thirsty for any drop of drama, not having many friends in the city.

"Three days ago, I had a very unpleasant encounter. with an ex of mine." Maya thought about disclosing Elle's identity but decided that would stir too much drama, knowing the hospital often got called to assist Elle's department. Rumors fly round fast in this town, that's for sure. She scoffed. "She thinks she still could have a chance."

Fleur smiled. "Could she?"

Maya immediately flushed. "No. What? She made an idiot out of me. She may have impressed me when I was twenty, but I'm too old and wise for women like her now."

"What kind of a person is she?"

. . .

Maya opened her mouth to answer, but an ER medic burst in.

"Dr. Monroe? We have a major incident, we need all trauma surgeons on board right now. We're sending you out to the scene." And he was gone.

Maya immediately rose to her feet and ran to the ambulances being dispatched. The paramedics and surgeons swarmed around the cars, getting in as fast as humanly possible.

A MAJOR CAR PILE UP ON HIGHWAY 65A, 15 MILES IN welcomed her as she quickly got ready to depart. The driver adjusted her seat, and at once they were on their way.

The usual adrenaline rush while speeding through the city with sirens ringing around her head caused Maya's thoughts to run at three times the speed as fast as usual. Images and fragments of conversations marched onto the fast beating of her heart, and she couldn't stop herself from wondering whether she'd see Elle on the scene. The thought grew so itchy that she couldn't even tell whether she'd like the idea or not. Elle's charming smile and seductive dark green eyes like a dark and mysterious forest flashed into her mind. *I wouldn't,* she kept telling herself while feeling it wasn't entirely true. Her stomach twisted and tied knots around her confidence, shaking the belief held for years that she was entirely over Elle.

"Hey, Maya." The surgeon in charge of her team patted her shoulder. "I don't know what you're thinking about, but remember not to bring it to the scene, all right? We have a lot of shit to do there." he nodded, seeking a *yes*.

"Yes, of course." Maya straightened up on her seat, prepared to cast aside any personal feelings and plunge straight into action. They were approaching the scene.

. . .

The massacred cars piling up on the asphalt made Maya's blood run cold. The ambulances already in action had nothing to spare in time or staff. Crowds of firefighters lifted cars up and pulled people crashed beneath them in terrifying numbers.

The team got out, running up to the nearest firefighter chief as they sought to coordinate efforts. They positioned themselves nearby a cluster of cars and received the first victims.

Maya quickly received a victim of blunt force trauma and began working on saving his life. Whenever she laid her hands on an injured person, everything around her quieted down. She became completely engrossed in the task at hand no matter how loud or chaotic the surroundings. When the victim's condition was stabilized and he'd been driven off to the hospital, she received another one, and in the brief moment in between, she watched all her colleagues doing the same — fighting the widely spread threat of death amidst the wreckage of cars. She felt the familiar sense of flow and dove right back to work.

Maya thrived in these situations, calm in a crisis, talented with her hands, highly skilled, and a natural problem solver.

It was a shame she seemed unable to apply any of her talents to her love life.

After a few more patients, she received instructions to collaborate more closely with the firefighters who were working on freeing a large group from a crashed van. She and her colleague took their medical bags and ran up to the team.

The firefighter standing at the forefront of the efforts to leverage the van wore a jacket that clearly read RODRIGUEZ, but Maya had no time to think about her grudges with Elle. There were lives to save beneath that van, and she stood ready to give the best assistance she could to save the stuck people. With a deep groan, Elle and her colleagues managed to lift the van and remove the family from the treacherous metal grasp.

Maya's heart sank, seeing two little children covered in blood. They quickly placed everyone on stretchers and the group of medics ran back close to the ambulance, ready to operate. She had to call a pediatric surgeon for support. The boys couldn't be older than three years old, and the anatomy and physiology of a small child was wildly out of Maya's field.

They managed to send everyone to the hospital still breathing. Maya went around the ambulances to check whether they needed help, and of course, they did. A few victims died and had to be removed from the stretchers to make space for the living.

The groups of firefighters and medical teams pulsed around the scene in a harmonized effort resembling that of a living organism. Maya knew her place and responsibility within it just as well as Elle, and they kept the rescue going like a pair of blood cells travelling within veins to and from the beating heart. Sometimes, their respective efforts would bring them closer to each other as if on a tidal wave, and Maya, seeing the jacket RODRIGUEZ somewhere in her peripheral view, grew more secure. Whatever Elle was in her romantic life had no impact on her skills as a firefighter. She remained stone-calm under any amount of pressure and took care to infect her entire team with it, engaging whatever hell they were facing with a collected and sharp mind.

After an exhausting fight with death, Maya was replaced by another surgeon as her shift came to an end. She'd been on the scene for more than ten hours, and her mind felt like a buzzing swarm of needles ready to tear apart her skull.

Her colleagues drove her and a bunch of other nearly passing out doctors back to the hospital so they could collect their cars and get home. Maya was desperate for a shower and some food.

. . .

In the parking lot, Maya realized she was in no state to drive home. She approached one of the taxis waiting next to the hospital and requested a ride home. On the passenger seat, watching the city's landscape blur with the car's increasing speed, her mind drifted toward the solid work she'd done. Elle's presence hadn't impacted her own work, at least, but her mind still felt so screwed up by the day as a whole.

For Maya, it took more time to get used to the constant hurricane of tragedy. She'd become a surgeon because she cared deeply about helping people, and her precise memory coupled with razor-sharp focus made her a truly perfect surgeon. Whenever she had a human body under her scalpel, she stopped seeing them as a human being, and she became a surgeon. She was only the pair of hands steadily wielding the tools and her knowledge of anatomy, whatever she was operating was just that, a tangle of nerve endings, bones, joints, skin, something she knew how to fix, how to make functional again, or at least prevent from collapsing.

. . .

But especially at the beginning, as soon as she looked around, she saw the true face of tragedy. Bodies dragged around on the pavement, patients dying on her hands, buildings burning, and cars crashed to pieces with entire families inside of them. Emergency workers grow used to it, but never entirely. Otherwise they'd lose their humanity.

Elle was made to be an emergency worker, and Maya had always admired her mental strength. Or at least, what she saw as mental strength. Ever since high, school Elle had been fearless. Nonchalant and slightly distant in her daily life, during emergencies she behaved as if no amount of emotional charge could deter her from seeing things crystal clear.

Despite that, she never patronized Maya for her emotions at the beginning of their professional journeys. She was the most supportive person in Maya's surroundings. In fact, on her free days, she'd stayed up until late hours to welcome her home, listen to her stories, and hear about the pain she'd witnessed. Elle's training rarely required her to witness real disasters. At first she'd been called to minor incidents and mainly stayed at the station training. For Maya, as a surgeon, it had been very different. She saw death and the threat of it day in, day out, and nearing the end of her second year of practice, she was as close as ever to burning out.

She remembered particularly vividly one night from that period—

A patient she'd been tasked to operate on called her in, seemingly to consult something regarding the surgery. She'd come in alone. The patient was an elderly woman, though younger than Maya's grandma. Maya quickly recognized the woman was in a state of delirium, progressing rapidly. She called a nurse and another doctor. Before she'd managed to do anything herself, the woman began violently gasping for air and reaching to hold on to something, her heartbeat thudding like crazy. Maya knew the woman was experiencing a heart attack, but before she'd managed to take a hold of her, the patient had fallen from the bed and had hit her head hard against the rim of her nightstand. She'd suffered a fatal bleed on the brain.

. . .

The experience had left Maya in shock. The fellow doctors had sent her for a consultation with a psychologist, the first one in her life. Her family came from too poor a background to afford any mental health services. Sitting in a wide leather chair, he announced her unable to continue practice until she got proper therapeutic help. She went home shattered, unable even to cry. There was nothing that could help her afford therapy.

That night, Elle had been on duty until two in the morning, and Maya sat on the couch unable to move. The sight of the blood on the floor replayed continuously in her mind to the point of complete numbness. She was afraid she'd lose her senses.

Elle finally came home, her sweat-soaked tank top and defined muscles constantly in movement, bringing such a strong wave of life into the room that Maya's eyes welled with tears. Elle came up to her with her casual *what's the matter?* expression. She'd been a great partner to lean on in those situations because she never made an unnecessarily big deal out of anything, providing sober and stable support.

"What's up?" She took Maya in her arms, enveloping her in the familiar scent of her skin, the sweet familiarity of her sweat, and the faint odor of fire that always clung to her.

For a long time, no answer emerged from Maya's lips. They simply stood in the middle of their shabby flat, Elle gently rocking them both side to side. After a while, Maya started crying.

"A woman died today right in front of me," she said, sobbing. Elle only nodded in response.

Maya gestured for them to sit down, exhausted both mentally and physically. For a long time they sat glued to each other while Elle kept stroking Maya's hair. Elle's chest's steady rhythm reassured Maya in some subtle but vital way.

. . .

"I broke down. I've never seen anything so bad before. I couldn't do anything. I couldn't save her. There was blood. So much blood," she finally found the words to say.

Elle's chest kept rising and falling, the eternal rhythm of life against Maya's cheek. They both knew there wasn't much to say to that, no words that could remedy something so very innately human.

"They said," Maya continued after a while, "that I need psychological support if I want to continue practice." She looked at Elle. "I can't afford that."

"But you want to continue?"

"Of course."

. . .

"Even if it keeps being like this? It will keep being like this, you know."

"I know." Maya inhaled deeply. "But it's worth it. Because I'll get better at what I do. And I'll save people."

In the weeks following that night, Maya had contacted every single friend who specialized in mental health she could think of, only to learn that she couldn't have an acquaintance as her therapist. Miraculously, it turned out that one of Elle's old friends had switched careers and was a practicing psychologist. After a few meetings, he couldn't refuse – no one could refuse Elle's charisma, after all, especially at that time.

Maya could still remember the smug smile on Elle's face when she broke the news to her.

"Your therapy sessions start at 7 p.m. Wednesday, the same time each week, so you'd better break it to your superiors that they need to clear your schedule for the time slot," she casually mentioned while frying eggs on their crusty old pan.

"What? That's not funny, Elle, I--"

"I'm serious, Maya. You've got this," she grinned. "Remember Albert?"

"No?" She crossed her arms, sure this would turn into a joke, and into an unfunny one at that.

"Sure you do. He was it high school math classes with me." Elle made fake glasses out of her fingers, "the really geeky one who was in love with me, remember?"

And it had indeed turned out not to be a joke. On said Wednesday, Maya started her mandated therapy for free, thanks to some long-forgotten high school admirer of Elle's. Or so she'd believed, until she found out that Elle was secretly paying for it (although at half the price), and the information infuriated Maya.

A hand gently touched her shoulder, and Maya realized she'd been thinking with her eyes closed, in a state of half-sleep. The driver kindly pointed to her house.

"Here we are, ma'am."

She dragged herself out of the low-set car and climbed the steps to her temporary apartment like a person who's half-alive. The vivid memories still popped up in her thoughts from time to time, and she almost expected to open the door to her old studio flat she'd shared with Elle in their early twenties.

She knew she should be calling her agent to check the state of the paperwork before his office closed for the day, but nothing seemed less appealing to her at the moment, so she decided to finally shower, eat something, and simply go to sleep.

Upon opening the fridge, she realized she hadn't gone shopping. The carton of half a dozen eggs, zucchini, and a bottle of ketchup constituted such a sad image that she closed the fridge. In the freezer she found a pack of ravioli and settled the matter.

While waiting for the ravioli to cook, she remembered what a great cook she'd once been. On the rare occasions when both she and Elle had been free from work, she could sit for hours in the kitchen accompanied by Elle and often some other friend or two. She'd revived her old family recipes, experimented, and had, overall, had incredible fun.

After moving to Forest Vale, she'd gotten so sucked into work that she could barely find time for any semblance of a social life, much less sitting for hours to stir sauces and watch pastries grow in the oven. Sometimes, Sylvia would bring her university friends over for baking parties, or at least to drunkenly try making pizza from scratch.

Maya hated the mess they'd always make, but undeniably, she also felt a pang of jealousy that those days were long gone. And, piled together with the feeling of an irreversible loss of the chance for a slower life lay the uncomfortable fact that she had not been in love since Elle. No torture method could make Maya admit that to anyone, especially not to Elle herself.

She'd dated other women, sure, but it had never gotten to the point where she could say they were in *love.*

After splitting up with Elle, she was so full of rage and hurt pride that she'd quickly plunged into a "glow-up phase," at least as much as her job allowed her to. She got a Jane Birkin inspired hairstyle (which, she learned, was entirely impractical for a surgeon due to the fringe and had to painfully wait for it to grow out), a new wardrobe, and new friends. She felt hot, she felt daring, she felt as if she'd wasted her whole youth dating one person.

But that phase had quickly passed. Maya had learned that most people her age were looking for quick hookups or non-committal relationships, and she really wasn't made for that. Her enthusiasm quickly burnt out, and once again she became completely engrossed in her career. She took on additional hours and limited her outings to a small bunch of friends. In Forest Vale she dated a few women, but the relationships alway dissolved quickly, and she realized how limited the lesbian dating circle was in a smaller town.

The sound of her kitchen timer rang out, pulling her out of the stream of thought.

Enough reminiscing, she declared, digging a fork into the sauce-covered squares.

5

ELLE

The kid just did not want to get down.

Elle's department had been called in to rescue a little boy stuck in a tall tree. At first, Elle thought it was a joke. Nothing like this had happened in her whole career. Roofs? Yes. Absolutely. A tree? That sounded like another made up story of firefighters rescuing a cat.

When they got on the scene, though, Elle understood the problem. The tree looked enormous, and the first half of it had no branches on w hich to climb.

"How did he even get up there?" she asked, half-amazed, half utterly surprised.

His shaken mother rushed in with explanations, while Captain Hunter organized the ladder to be put against the tree. There was some issue with the placement of their truck due to the neighboring houses standing very tightly knit.

"He and his sister found an old, wooden ladder in our garage, but when he let go of it after climbing up the tree, it fell and broke in half." She pointed to the broken ladder lying in the corner of the garden.

"And what were their parents doing while the kids nearly got deadly injured?" Chastising irresponsible parents had to be Elle's favorite leisure activity. "Why was the garage even left open for them to access?"

The mother furrowed her eyebrows, offended. "Well, I don't know whether you have kids of your own, ma'am." She looked Elle up and down. "But it's not that easy keeping a 24/7 watch over two kids under five."

"But you could close your garage, no?" Elle pointed to it still being open. "Or do you want us to come in next time to extinguish your burning house after one of your kids plays around with the gas bottles over there?"

She shook her head, leaving to join the team trying to convince the small boy not to wriggle around and let them do their job. His face was twisted with terrible fear, and he refused to do anything besides clutch onto the tree. O'Malley finally got close enough to capture him, but the challenge then lay in the boy not jerking away. Elle had no idea why Hunter had chosen O'Malley, as she had no skills with children whatsoever. The moment Elle thought this, the child started wailing so loudly even Hunter was clearly questioning her choice of firefighter for the job.

"For fuck's sake." She sighed, eyeing the parents angrily.

Finally, O'Malley managed to take a firm hold of the child. Everyone began clapping, relieved. The boy, having no other choice, clung close to her chest, and they both safely got to the ground.

The team worked smoothly to get the ladder back down and safely loaded back into its place on the truck.

"This has been the worst mission of my life," O'Malley muttered under her breath when passing Elle.

"Good job," Elle shouted, and mounted her seat as the fire truck's driver. "Let's go, everyone!"

Elle always liked driving the truck. It took real skill to drive a big truck at speed and avoid others on the road, and Elle prided herself on doing it well.

The four of them were quickly on their way back, apparently in a very talkative mood. Captain Hunter, Chief Ramirez, O'Malley and Elle. The day had a lazy feeling to it, and the clear sky put everyone in a good mood. Elle laughed heartily, though at the back of her mind swam something darker.

"You should never have kids, O'Malley." Chief Ramirez shook her head. "They're worse than a thousand fires."

Ramirez had two of her own, now well into adulthood. Sometimes her daughter would bring pastries to the station. She worked as a pastry chef in a local bakery. Easy to say, she was the delight of the entire station.

"Yeah, Chief, next time you try grabbing a crying, wriggling, snot-covered brat from a tree, we'll see how that goes."

"Oh, love, I've done that many, many times." Chief laughed, effectively shutting O'Malley up. The whole exchange didn't fail to make Elle laugh again.

"And you, keep your eyes on the road, huh?"

Ramirez snapped, and Elle shut her laugh down immediately.

Elle put two teaspoons of sugar in the steamy cup of coffee, then sat back down, facing Chief Ramirez. The two shared particularly amicable relations, being the only two Latinas in their department. From day one, Ramirez had taken special care of Elle, acting as a mentor figure throughout Elle's career. She knew Elle's mother had been rather absent, so she never hesitated to lift the young firefighter up.

"Hey, what's with you?" Ramirez put down the newspaper she'd been pretending to read.

"What? Nothing." Elle shrugged, taking a sip of her coffee.

"Oh don't play tough with me, Rodriguez."

Elle's lips stretched in a little smile disguised by the cup. Whenever Ramirez used her surname, she could feel how close they'd grown. She could sense that particular tone people familiar to you use when they put on formal words, the beating flesh of affection hidden by the formal attire they dressed it up in.

"I swear I'm not," Elle protested, but deep down she knew that Ramirez got her.

Her Chief only raised an eyebrow, waiting.

"Yes, something's wrong with me," Elle exhaled the air she didn't know she'd been trapping in her lungs.

"Go on," Rodriguez nodded.

"Someone I used to know is back in the city," she began, unsure of how to put in words what lay heavy on her chest, but willing to try. "Someone I cared about deeply. She's a doctor. I keep seeing her at incidents."

Rodriguez nodded patiently. "So where is the problem?"

"We didn't part on the best... terms. Actually, we parted on awful terms. We'd broken up before she moved away. Now she's back." Elle looked up at Rodriguez.

"And you don't want to be near her now?"

"No! I really do, actually. See, I realized that she's the only one I want."

Ramirez burst out laughing uncontrollably, waving her arms in what seemed to be a simultaneous apology. "I'm sorry! I'm sorry, but I find it very difficult to believe, Elle!"

Elle's expression turned sour. "Now why's

that?"

"Why's that? You go through women like plastic straws at a Malibu bar, sometimes three at a time." Ramirez calmed down. "Are you serious? What makes this one so special?"

"See, she was with me before all that." Elle's expression remained serious. "She was the only one I've ever actually fallen for. Like, truly. We grew up together. We were together for years. First love and all that."

Ramirez looked at Elle in disbelief. "Girl, you should have married her. I've never seen you like this."

Elle sighed. "If only you knew. She's all I want."

"So what's the problem? Why'd you break up?"

"I..." Elle braced herself for the unavoidable reaction from Ramirez. "I cheated on her."

Ramirez fell silent, nodding. "I see. Well, that is a mistake, for sure."

"I have a feeling that due to my...reputation, I may have made it harder for her down the line." Elle nodded ruefully.

"You very well might've."

"So I don't know what to do. She doesn't want me back." Elle looked at her superior, helpless.

"Girl, I wouldn't want you back either, no offense."

"Offense taken."

"Let me ask you this—have you actually grieved your relationship?" Ramirez posed the question with a serious expression on her face.

"What do you mean?" Elle seemed confused.

"Have you allowed yourself to actually feel the devastation? From what I can see, you never actually allowed yourself to feel the loss. And if you haven't felt the loss, you haven't had the chance to truly feel remorseful for what you did. The whole time I've known you, you've just been going through women. Oh, and drinking. You may want to take a look at the drinking, too. Think about it. What was the first thing you did after you two broke up?"

Elle thought for a moment. "I got laid."

Ramirez nodded. "And then?"

"I got laid again, because that one wasn't fulfilling."

"And I suppose you just kept going?"

"It's not that simple, okay? Of course I respect

all the women I've slept with, and wanted to have something with them, but--"

"Of course." Ramirez nodded. "But you never acknowledged the hurt you caused the person you loved most, so instead of going through a healthy process of grief and healing, you're just out here being a Casanova breaking hearts on repeat."

Elle giggled. "Is that how you look at me, really?"

"That's how you act, either way. You must allow yourself to feel the regret buried somewhere there in your stone-cold heart."

Elle opened her mouth to protest, but Ramirez shut her down. "I'm joking. I'm joking. Only don't get defensive. Think about it for a moment, maybe longer. You're charming as hell, Elle, but that won't get you very far with your ex. She already knows you, I'd guess even better than you yourself, kid. She needs you to actually work on yourself, not try to seduce her with the Rodriguez charm like all the others."

And having released this waterfall of knowledge, Ramirez got up and went to check on the new recruits.

Elle sat thoughtfully next to her cup of coffee for

a long time. Ramirez was one of the only people who could talk her down like that, call her a *kid*. Either way, her advice sounded difficult and unrewarding to Elle. Deep down, she knew Ramirez was right, she wished she could simply charm her way back to Maya's heart. And she knew Maya enough to know Maya still had feelings for her. That lip twitching, that particular flavor of emotions she'd seen rush through Maya during their argument, had told her all she wanted to know. Maya may hate her, but you had to still love someone in order to hate them. Elle knew that. She just had to somehow get Maya to switch back more to the love side of things.

Driving home, Elle couldn't understand the idea of feeling *supposed* emotions seven years after the fact. And for sure, she didn't understand how feeling grief would help her be a better girlfriend. The whole situation was about that one drunken mistake, and Elle would reverse all these seven years if she could, but she couldn't, and now she was driving her car to a huge, empty house with no one in it to welcome her, no trace of anyone who would love her.

Although at least she had a great house, and at least there was whiskey at her house.

These thoughts made her feel weak. Insecure.

Sorry for herself. Feeling sorry for herself was Elle's worst enemy. Other people could show their weaknesses just fine, but Elle's standard for herself had always been so high above that she sometimes lost sight of it, chasing something vaguely upward to no end. Not even a dog or cat to welcome her home. Elle loved animals, but her shifts were long, and she just knew it wouldn't be fair to take on a pet and not be home enough for it. So all she came home to was a racist neighbor and her screaming children. Not the kids' fault they were screaming. Elle would be screaming too if she had to live with that woman. Elle had always had a weak spot for children. Something about their untamed curiosity and flexibility of mind soothed her, aside their obvious gentleness.

No child could be truly cruel, and their presence made Elle feel safe. She had thought once that she'd have kids with Maya. But that hope of being a parent had died when Maya had left. No way working/womanizing/drinking Elle would make a fit parent, and she knew that. So when asked, she always said she didn't want kids.

Once home, she opened all the windows wide. She felt the need for air, to breathe in and out deeply, to release the pent up feeling of claustrophobia left from her conversation with Ramirez. She remembered distinctly how Maya would do that to let fresh air into their apartment, sometimes forgetting to close them overnight, and causing them both to wake up cold. After a while, Elle learned to wake up in the middle of the night to go around their flat and check whether all the windows had been closed. For a while after their breakup she'd still do that, startling an occasional hookup, but over the years the habit had faded away.

The memory made her feel deep sadness, an emotion she normally wouldn't dwell upon, but this time, trying to follow Ramirez's advice, she took up a pen from her desk.

I feel deep sadness.

She wrote on a piece of paper, silently swearing to herself she'd start a journal and keep it secret from everyone. Not that it would be difficult, living on her own.

I love Maya,

For the rest of the evening, she sat scribbling away. Simple statements about her day, about her feelings, things she hadn't admitted to anyone for ages, if ever. A chaotic sprawl of feeling, but in a good way. Emotions she had no idea were nested in her mind after the day of work made their way onto the page, sometimes in clumsy words or incoherent sentences, but the activity brought her some unexpected peace of mind.

She finished writing with one sentence at the bottom of the page:

"Now my father would say I am weak.

6

MAYA

The ambulance sirens screamed above Maya's head with what seemed to her an unusual intensity. In the intimate space of the car, the crew's faces shared the same grim look. Once they'd get out on the scene, they would plunge into work, giving into the years of practice and rigorous training, foregoing whatever emotions might bubble beneath the surface. But for the few moments they had within the walls of the ambulance, they had time for themselves.

The scene was a high school bus accident.

. . .

The bus lay on its side, crumpled like a mere yellow napkin. The road had been entirely shut off, causing waves of dissatisfied drivers to honk at the barriers until they got closer and saw the disaster. Maya saw sheets covering the dead who had already been recovered. Maya saw another team quickly collecting their bodies and preparing to drive away, hurrying partially out of respect, partially so as not to make a spectacle. Maya hated when the passersby made a private show out of tragedy—when they'd slow down just to look, to catch a glimpse of a body or a massacred car. Natural human curiosity, some strange proclivity for seeking out terrible images, she knew that was unavoidable, and yet... Her blood boiled at the sight of gaping faces passing by the fences.

Maya and her colleagues set up the stretchers and waited for the firefighters to get more people out. It was clear not many would come out alive. The bus had fallen from a great height and one of its walls had been entirely caved in. This was a real tragedy and Maya steeled herself for what she was likely to experience. Suddenly the crew began moving around with heightened urgency – they pulled out a girl, still breathing and even conscious. Maya and a paramedic rushed to take her, and at once she understood there was a chance to save the teen. She quickly began stabilizing her. Maya worked quickly and was satisfied with her work, The girl was stable and was loaded into an ambulance. Another pair of ambulances arrived. The girl was driven off. Another teen victim made his way to Maya.

His rich, curly hair was clumped with dry blood, he had suffered trauma to his head and his chest was on the edge of bleeding out. Maya knew she had to act here and now and perform a surgery to stop the bleeding. He didn't have long. He wouldn't make it to the hospital. Only then had she noticed – she knew the boy. Looking at his face, she clearly recognized a shadow of another one, a very familiar one. Her hands began shaking. Should she call out for someone else to help?

Oh god, it was her nephew. Her brother's son Alexei.

. . .

Her nephew lay unconscious, and she couldn't move. Then, she realized there was no one better for the job on the scene. If she wanted to save Alexei, she had to act immediately. She drew a deep breath and began working, trying to treat his body like any other she'd have no issues mending. Her hands trembled more than usual, but Maya worked quickly.

She had to save him. She had to.

Performing any kind of surgery here at the roadside was a risk, but it was his only chance.

With the help of the paramedic, Maya made progress and Alexei's condition improved. She thought he was stable enough to move, although certainly not out of the woods yet. The ambulance left quickly to get Alexei to the OR where hopefully they could save him.

Maya remembered him when he was a little boy. Blond curly hair, a curious little personality.

. . .

Please, please, please. Save Alexei.

Once her emotional state no longer had effect upon Alexei's chances of survival, Maya began breathing heavily. Her legs seemed to bend in strange ways beneath her, and dizziness haunted her head. She'd never operated upon family before, and the pressure she'd felt was the reason why. Her eyes watered while she searched for her brother's number in her phone. As soon as she heard the familiar deep voice, she felt the horrible burden of being the bearer of bad news.

"Colin, listen." She took in a deep breath. "Alexei has been in an accident. He's on his way to Phoenix Ridge Hospital. He'll need to go straight into surgery, so head to the ER."

"What? What happened, Maya?"

"I hope he will be okay..." She couldn't stop the tears from falling down her face, and her throat seemed too tight to let out coherent words. "I operated on him, and now he's in the ambulance on the way to hospital..."

She promised to visit as soon as they didn't need her on the scene anymore, but the team had already realized something had happened to Maya and had decided to work without her for as long as necessary. They retrieved the last pair of kids from under the bus, and their job on the scene seemed to be finished.

Maya quickly wiped her eyes, completely overwhelmed.

"Are you okay?"

The familiar voice shot through Maya like a bullet. She didn't have to move to know who it was. She didn't have to look. She'd recognize this voice anywhere she'd go, still, she decided to slowly turn around and put on an air of complete nonchalance.

"Oh, it's you." Maya crossed her arms. "Yeah, I'm fine."

"This was intense."

Maya's eyebrows raised in an incredulous look. There was no way she'd allow Elle to use a tragedy like this to advance her own selfish goals. Not after Alexei had almost lost his life.

"What do you want?"

Elle knitted her eyebrows in a confused expression. "What do I want? I don't know, you were crying, you shouted for help that one time, so I wanted to check in on you since none of your teammates did." She looked around to prove the point, then raised her hands. "That's it."

. . .

"Do you think I'm dumb? I know what you're doing, and frankly, it's disgusting."

"I think you're getting a bit ahead of yourself." Elle took a step toward Maya. "What's this really about?"

"No, stop it with the patronizing voice, all right? I'm not a child. Nor am I twenty anymore. I'm not just another one of your *girls,* Elena," she spat.

"Maya, stop it." Elle wiped the sweat off her forehead. "You won't even let me say what I came here to say, and you're once again accusing me of something random. I don't even know what you've heard--"

At this, Maya scoffed. Elle continued talking.

. . .

"And I just wanted to say that I'm sorry. I'm sorry for what I've done, I'm sorry for how our relationship ended, and I'm sorry how others treated you afterward, even though it wasn't my fault."

"Are you finished now?"

"Yes?" Elle spread her arms, "Was that not clear?"

Maya felt as if her blood was on fire. She couldn't stand how Elle thought everything could be fixed by saying a few words, making an appearance, and looking sexy as hell. She knew this was Elle's way of getting through life and stood as determined as ever to prove her wrong, to prove that some things aren't fixable. That one cannot push back time, no matter how charming or confident or beautiful they are. The gravel beneath her feet squeaked when she came up closer to Elle's beautiful face and clear green eyes. Elle's dark wavy hair was in a messy ponytail.

She was close enough to kiss, and Maya had to

do everything she could to hold back her lips from moving impulsively.

"I'm not a toy that you can break and then glue back together on a whim, Elena. I won't come running back to you because you said you're *sorry*. Did you think you could just charm your way back, wear your old cologne scent on your neck, flash your perfect smile, and have me swoon over you? I know you. I *knew* you, and you don't seem to have gotten better. If anything you've gotten worse since the last time I saw you. You don't think about anyone besides yourself. Have you ever considered that maybe I'm happy now? Without you?"

Elle stood quietly, looking at Maya with the soft, wounded green eyes of a kicked puppy. "Who said I wanted to go back to you?"

"I did. I see what you're doing. Look me in the eyes and tell me I'm wrong." Maya came closer to Elle's face, so close their noses almost touched. "Look me in the eyes and tell me that's not what you're trying to do."

"Maya." Elle's voice cracked with tension.

Elle's dark green eyes sparkled dangerously as she slowly shook her head left to right, then pressed her lips to Maya's.

Maya kissed her back.

Elle's strong arms took a hold of Maya and Elle's tongue pushed into her mouth. Maya heard herself moan involuntarily.

Fuck.

Maya didn't know what she wanted, didn't know what she was doing, but Elle's lips on hers, her strong arms, the taste of her, felt too daring not to accept.

Elle bit her lip, pushing Maya against the back wall of the ambulance. Maya put her fingers deep into Elle's hair and felt Elle's knee pushing her thighs open. She gasped but followed the direction and spread her legs, letting Elle nest her thigh in between Maya's, pressing against her clitoris.

Then, Maya suddenly sobered up. She abruptly pushed Elle away, wiping her mouth and putting herself back in order. Her thoughts spun in a tangle of guilt, afraid she'd sent Elle the wrong signal, upset at disrespecting her own boundaries and emotions.

"I hate you," she whispered. "Please go away."

Elle, confused, backed away. Her mouth formed a delicate prideful smile. "You don't hate me, Maya."

. . .

"Go away, Elena."

Finally, Elle turned around on her heel and walked away. Once her back became lost among the other firefighters, Maya allowed herself to breathe. She felt sick. Her tongue still held onto Elle's taste despite all her best efforts. Disgust at herself bubbled wildly in her stomach. The medics began getting into the ambulances, waving at her to join them.

"Hey, Maya, everything all right? Where'd you go?" Maya's colleague touched her back in a friendly gesture.

"I'm sorry, Richard, I just... I know one of the kids."

He went pale. "But not one of the...?"

"No! No. I stabilized him myself, and he went off to the hospital."

. . .

"Jesus Christ, how'd you manage that? You should've called for someone else."

Maya shook her head. "You were all busy. It was fine. I'm fine now."

Richard nodded. "You know, you can always talk to me, or any other doctor on our team. We're here for each other. It's not easy work."

Maya nodded, grateful for the unexpected support.

Her thoughts raced around, each heavy and dangerous like gasoline trucks all on a collision course with each other. She radioed the hospital, gaining an update on Alexei. Stable. Out of surgery. At least, she knew now Alexei lay safe in a hospital bed, none of his injuries causing a direct threat to his life. She had no idea how to tackle the situation with Elle. She wished she could open the door to that moment of the lapse in her judgement and jerk herself away from Elle, shake herself awake. That sorry apology wasn't worth two cents. It definitely wasn't worth leaning in to kiss the offender. Maya buried her head in her hands, still smelling of the strong alcohol disinfectant.

On her way to the hospital to see Alexei, Maya's phone rang. She turned her head to see the number and froze. She hadn't seen it for years, and liked to think she wouldn't recognize it anymore. Oh, how wrong she'd been.

"Where'd you get my number?"

"I...remember it."

Maya smiled, though she quickly chastised herself for it.

"I think I've been very clear, I don't want anything to do with you, Elena."

. . .

"Yeah, I got that message exactly from having your tongue in my mouth."

A little giggle made to sound mechanical by the speaker system filled Maya's car. She sighed, gathering herself up together.

"What I did was immature and unfair to you. I acknowledge that."

"*I acknowledge that* is so in your style to say," Elle interrupted. "You clearly want me."

"Maybe I do. But it isn't healthy, I don't feel good about us seeing each other. I don't feel good about you. I think I made that sufficiently clear. I hope you find someone who'll want you, Elena. That's not going to be me. Bye."

. . .

Maya hung up. The conversation had drained her, leaving her mind dry, sore, empty of any reason, like a desert. The car smelled of citrus air freshener, which greatly irritated her nose. Everything felt out of place and hopeless, but at last she arrived at the hospital's parking lot, overcrowded as always.

"Maya." Colin spread his arms wide, inviting her in for a hug. His woodsy perfume always filled her with a deep sense of comfort, like bed sheets wrapped around a sleeping child.

"Hi," she whispered, setting her forehead against his chest. "Did he wake up at all?"

"Yes, but he quickly went back to sleep. The nurses say he's in a lot of pain when he's awake, so they gave him a mild sedative. It's better to let him sleep."

Of course." Maya sighed with relief. "It's so good to hear he woke up this soon."

So as not to disturb the boy, Maya and Colin went down to the hospital cafeteria. Maya stirred sugar into her watery coffee, and steam blew in her face. All around, parents, children, and spouses nervously struggled with their lukewarm meals. The food here was terrible. It wasn't just Maya's dietary requirements that meant she usually brought her own with her. The harsh light hurt her eyes.

"How have you been, Maya?" Colin touched her arm. His eyes bore dark circles underneath.

"I don't know. I don't even know where to start." Maya shook her head. "Tell me about you."

"Pfff. Daniele is getting married." Colin smiled. "I got invited to the wedding."

. . .

Maya laughed, the tight strained type of laughter that escapes a stress-ridden mouth, a tired mouth. Maya felt exhausted. "Are you serious?"

"I mean, we've been friends for a while now. It's fine."

"I don't know how you always end up friends with your exes. It's crazy to me." Maya took a sip of the coffee, shaking her head.

She was desperately trying not to talk about herself, but every thought led her back to Elle. The dangerous curve of her lips and their charming smile.

Quickly, she decided to change the subject, or at least drive it safely away from exes. "And are you seeing anyone new?"

. . .

"No. Honestly, I have no time for dating. The job, together with Alexei, fill up all my time." He paused, worry about his son creasing his face. "I hope he'll be out of here soon."

"He will." Maya took his hand. "I swear, kids heal at an insane rate. Three weeks and he'll be out."

"It's been so difficult with him recently. They all say that's just a phase with teenagers, but I swear, parenting him on my own is on another level. I've read like three parenting books this year already."

Maya smiled, trying to imagine Colin sitting with a parenting textbook in his hand. "You're a very good father. I'm sure he'll be just fine. He's very lucky to have you."

"And then I think…" Colin hesitated, "I sometimes think the divorce might have affected him. You know, like I think when our parents divorced, well, that wasn't …easy on you."

. . .

"What's that supposed to mean?" Maya straightened up in her chair.

"I was old enough not to care, but don't you think it made certain things difficult for you?"

"Like what, Colin?" The nerve in her neck began pulsing slightly, she wanted him to finish what he'd started.

"You know what I'm talking about."

"No, like what?" Maya sat straight as an arrow, tense, looking into Colin's eyes.

"Like relationships, Maya."

For a few moments they sat in complete silence, chewing the sentence in their minds. Maya kept biting her nails and could see how hard Colin was trying not to comment on that. She did it more viciously out of spite.

"Says the divorced one," she finally forced herself to respond.

"Yes, peacefully ending my marriage of twelve years because we grew apart," he muttered, before adding "it's not about you being single."

Maya raised an eyebrow, swearing at herself for allowing the conversation to turn this way. They could never discuss her love life peacefully.

"Well, how do you view this, then? Are you happy?" Colin spread his arms in surrender.

She looked at him, surprised. There was not one mocking note in his voice. His question had been asked, she knew, with pure intentions. That undid her defensive pose.

"I miss her."

Colin's face softened. He knew exactly who she was talking about. "Have you seen her since you've been back?"

Maya nodded.

"And?" Colin's face was open and kind. He'd always liked Elle. But he also knew how much she'd hurt Maya.

"I don't think she fully understands how betrayed I felt. How hurt I still feel. And she didn't reach out all these years... And as soon as I come back, she wants to prove something to herself, maybe, and get me to want her again."

. . .

"You have a very harsh idea of her intentions already, don't you?" Colin shook his head. "Maybe it wouldn't hurt to give her a chance?"

Maya furrowed her eyebrows, "What if it isn't her I miss? What if I only miss being in love? Maybe there's someone else in my future. Another love. A better love. Someone who can love me back in the way I deserve to be loved?"

"No one can decide that for you, unfortunately."

They sat still for a few moments, listening to the people hustling around. The cafeteria emptied out a bit, the crowd slowly leaked out of the door one family after another.

She put her hand on top of Colin's, so much bigger rougher and hairier than her own. Her big brother had always been such a reassuring presence for her. She hoped she could reassure him now that his son was in trouble.

Meanwhile, as hard as she tried to fight it, her

own mind was persistently haunted with thoughts of Elle.

7

ELLE

The harsh, blue light was hitting Elle's sore eyes, but she couldn't put the phone down. Twisting in the sheets made hot by her skin, she feverishly kept swiping. Left, right, left, left, right, right, right, she made the dating app into a game, a game she wasn't sure she knew how to win.

Following the last encounter with Maya, however much heat had been in that kiss, Elle had decided: she would no longer be running around, chasing Maya Monroe like a loyal dog. This time, having been literally pushed away, and after that hung up on, she had lost her patience. She was not a teenager chasing around high school crushes, she thought, but a grown woman with lots to offer. And if Maya was not ready to grant her forgiveness, Elle wouldn't be simply sitting around, waiting.

Plenty of women wanted Elle Rodriguez and that hadn't changed.

Love is not that hard to find, she reasoned. All these women want me. I just need to find a way to be more open with them. To not keep running away from them as soon as I get them.

Another match. She liked this game, collecting women one by one, women who thought she were worth meeting. A match with someone named Rose.

Really hot, Elle sent the first message followed up with a fire emoji.

Unmatched, the screen read. Oh well.

Her loss.

Another match, this one particularly inviting- Louisa. Elle looked through all her photos; she was very pretty with sparkling brown eyes and blonde hair that reminded her frustratingly of Maya's own deep brown eyes and blonde hair. She was a bit younger than Elle, working as a chef. They exchanged a few messages, it looked promising.

Up for a dinner together next week? Elle clicked "send."

With pleasure, Darling Louisa responded.

Finally, Elle turned the phone off, casting it somewhere far away. The living room, in its spacious luxury, sometimes made her feel particularly soulless. Its large windows peered at the mowed lawns, and large, white surfaces of her furniture seemed to radiate a sad glow at night. She turned from side to side, fed up to the brim with her phone's light and unable to sleep.

There was no love in this house, she thought to herself.

Ever since the kiss with Maya, her thoughts had been haunted by erotic imaginings, threads of dreams mixed with glimmers of hope. It had been so long since she had been with Maya and they had both been so young. The only lingering feeling was that of absolute intimacy, something she chased afterwards and never managed to find again.

With other women since Maya, she had attained such a level of skill sexually in just about every way there was for two women to have sex. Elle's fingers tongue and strap could give pleasure in ways she had never known last time she had been with Maya.

Elle had women begging her to have sex with them one more time.

But, they had never felt the same. They lacked the emotional depth, they were acts of quick consumption.

The kiss with Maya had brought her blood to a boiling point, overcome her body with lust, made her understand what it could be like, if they were to make love again.

She shook her head, wanting to separate her thoughts by physically casting them away.

No, she wanted a new chapter. Maya had rejected every single advance she had made.

Surely this Louisa would fix up Elle's heart.

And holding that hope dearly to her chest, Elle slowly fell asleep.

"You're a chef, what would you recommend?" Elle put on her most charming voice, hoping to convince herself this had been a good idea.

Louisa's storm of short, curly blonde hair caught colorful specks of light reflected off of the restaurant's windows. She looked energetic and accompanied her words with vivid hand gestures.

"Hm... Probably Magret de Canard, since we're at a French restaurant something involving a duck would be recommended," she smiled. "I'm taking Poulet a la Provencale, I've been craving proper chicken!"

Elle felt herself quickly warming up to Louisa. The atmosphere was relaxed despite it being the first meeting, Elle didn't have to try that hard, and

Louisa's occupation as a chef intrigued Elle, as something so very far from her own career... and as with pretty much all firefighters, Elle was a huge fan of eating food.

"I've never talked to a firefighter before," Louisa swirled her wine with a knowing fluency of her wrist.

Elle raised her eyebrows, "what are your thoughts then, am I up to your expectations?"

Louisa deliberately looked her up and down with a hungry look in her eyes and Elle preened. She knew she looked good. She always looked good. "Exceeding them."

Their dishes arrived, fragrant and steamy. The silence that followed interrupted only by their chewing and sounds of cutlery, let Elle plunge into thought.

Something strange lay in sweet talking each

other so very explicitly. As Elle dug her fork into the duck, she thought of the delicious tension of uncertainty. The dance, as she called it. The push and pull of desire. Where was the space for that on dates such as this one? The only uncertainty that remained was *when* not *if*. There was no chase, and what Elle liked about dating, or sex, was the chase. *Do you want me the same way I want you?* was a question she could spend an eternity looking for the answer to.

Instead, she and Louisa had known what they came here for from the beginning. If there was no difficulty achieving affection, Elle reasoned, it would make sense for it to feel hollow, undeserved, expendable. Easily obtainable from someone else. But, she didn't want to lose hope. Perhaps after a while, it would start feeling entirely natural, perhaps they'd forget where they met.

"Thanks for recommending me this, it actually tastes insane," Elle nodded with approval, "should we go out for a smoke and get dessert?"

. . .

"Sure," Louisa laid her cutlery down, getting ready to step out onto the terrasse.

"So, why'd you decide to become a firefighter?" Louisa lit her cigarette off of Elle's, leaning in very close to her face.

"Oh, I just knew I'd be very good at it."

"Cocky," Louisa laughed. "Why'd you think so?"

Elle put her arm around Louisa's shoulders, feeling the fleece jacket against her skin. She took a moment to gather her thoughts, then responded, "I have always felt confident in dangerous situations. Focused." She looked at Louisa, smiling, "At peace, perhaps."

"That's quite deep. To feel at peace in danger."

. . .

Elle shrugged. "Yeah, well, I was right, wasn't I? I'm quite good at what I do."

"I wouldn't know," Louisa giggled, "you could be the worst firefighter on Earth, and I'd have no clue."

"Right," Elle nodded.

They stood closer to each other now, and Elle could recognize Louisa's perfume. Its zesty scent felt pleasant, though quite strong.

"You like strong perfume, hm?" She leaned in to gently touch Louisa's neck with her lips. She made her way up to her mouth, and laid a soft kiss on it. Louisa quietly sighed with unexpected pleasure.

"I like you for sure," she whispered.

. . .

They went back inside and ordered chef's apple pie for Louisa, a tiramisu for Elle, and another round of wine. With drinking, their voices gradually lowered and became husky, pleasantly contrasting with the clinking surroundings.

"Was it difficult, changing countries?" Elle had never been to Europe, nor any other continent for that matter, and Louisa's upbringing greatly interested her.

"At first there were some cultural shocks, big and small. Especially in the industry... She waved her hands in an abstract gesture, "but nothing too difficult to adjust to, I think at the end of the day, for our generation it's all the same."

Elle nodded. "I'd love to visit France some day, it sounds lovely."

"Well, prepare for the rats... Oh, and not a single person I know there can drive."

. . .

"How do you guys move around?" For Elle, driving had been her great freedom. Her first real taste of freedom, and her most treasured skill. To be able to go wherever she wanted, wherever her car would take her.

"Public transport and our feet," Louisa giggled, "I also only got my license here, I had no use for it before. Say whatever you want about Europe, but it's great to walk around."

"Maybe," Elle shrugged. She still struggled to imagine not owning a car. "In my department, I'm often the fire truck driver."

"Sounds stressful."

"It is, but as I told you, I work great under stress. Nerves made of steel."

. . .

"That would make you amazing in the kitchen," Louisa nodded, "we have that in common."

They walked giggly and weak-legged from laughter to their cars. Over the course of their dinner, Elle began feeling truly comfortable around Louisa, and a part of her didn't want to take her home, which would inevitably alter their dynamic. A part of her wished they'd preserve this blissful state of getting to know each other, before moving anywhere further. But Elle wasn't the one to refuse, she knew she'd follow Louisa's suggestion if posed.

They leaned against Louisa's car in a prolonged kiss. Her hands began going up Elle's hips, but then Elle interrupted. "Should we get in?"

On their way to Louisa's flat, they didn't say much. Her car provided a cool shelter against the heat of summer coming into full bloom, and each of them plunged deep into her own thoughts. Elle tried not comparing this situation to that with Mimi. Her mind ran in circles, bumping from one woman in Elle's memories to another, blurring the lines between them, making her guess who had been who.

She turned on the radio, and Jeff Buckley's voice filled the car.

"Oh no, this is so sentimental," Louisa sighed, but did not switch the station.

Watching Louisa drift into her own land of memories, Elle realized how different dating felt in adulthood. As late teenagers, everyone had been more or less a blank canvas, still full of enthusiasm and ready to dive into fresh experiences. Back then, it felt refreshing to meet someone new.

As adults, everyone came with an ocean of experience locked away behind their eyes. Clunky luggage dragged from relationship to relationship, piling up, inaccessible in its entirety. Unpacking it would take years, or even decades. As adults, you couldn't really take each other in completely, indiscriminately.

The car parked in front of an old, red brick apartment complex.

"What a nice building," Elle said, unfastening her belt. "I wonder whether it follows all the fire safety precautions."

Louisa gave her a dead stare. "Are you kidding me?"

Elle shook her head, "no, really, only a few weeks ago I was called to extinguish a really similar one. What an action that was, I had to go in to save some people who got stuck-"

"Ok, maybe let's not talk about my building burning down, you know? I have enough anxiety at my job," and having said that, Louisa got out of the car.

"Whatever," Elle muttered and followed suit.

. . .

Louisa's apartment welcomed Elle with the familiar to the core of her bones ambience of a person living alone. There was nothing she could pinpoint exactly; perhaps the set up of the dining table, so clearly out of use, or the lingerie thrown on random furniture inside of her bedroom. She knew this atmosphere intimately because it was like being in her own house.

"Could I have a glass of water?" She asked, realizing how dry the wine had gotten her mouth.

Louisa disappeared into the kitchen. The apartment was small, colorful prints decorated the walls, and each room had a carpet spread on the floor. *Cozy* was the only word that came to Elle's mind. Louisa reemerged with two glasses of water. They hadn't turned on the light, and everything seemed taken out of a fever dream. Moonlight shone through the water.

. . .

"How do you like it?"

"The room? It's cute," Elle looked around. "You collect vinyls? That's cool."

She liked it when people collected things, no matter what type. It seemed slightly foreign to her, in a good way. Maya had always been too frugal to collect anything besides her own money, and Elle preferred to spend hers on different indulgences. Jeff Buckley certainly denominated Louisa's collection.

They began kissing, the night enveloping them in a dreamlike unreality, their gestures remained foreign and full of moony sensuality. Without turning the lights on, Elle continued with what she knew was expected. She gave to Louisa, but she kept her own underwear on- she didn't want Louisa touching her. She knew that at the moment there was only one person she wanted touching her.

And however hard she tried, she just couldn't get Maya Monroe out of her head.

Elle woke up in a foreign bed, wondering what had led her to it. She shuffled through the memories of the night, looking around for Louisa. She wasn't to be found in the bed. This annoyed Elle; she never liked being the second to wake up. She got up, collecting her scattered clothes off the floor, stretching out her back and rubbing her sleep-sticky eyes.

Louisa suddenly entered the room. She was fully dressed and ready to go, bag in her hand and shoes on her feet. Elle looked at her with disbelief.

"You could've woken me up, you do know that?" She grunted, putting on her pants.

"I hoped you'd wake up on your own, so I just took care of my own stuff while waiting," she smiled hurriedly, "I don't want to be rude, but I really need to leave for work soon."

. . .

"Sure," Elle nodded, made utterly uncomfortable. "Next time, tell me when you need to wake up before we fall asleep, alright?"

But Louisa was already in the bathroom, finishing putting on her makeup. The sun was peeking through the see-through curtains, and Elle remembered only then that her car was still parked in front of the restaurant. She pondered asking Louisa for a lift, but seeing how their morning was going, she decided against it.

On her way from the restaurant, Elle decided to stop by a bistro and buy herself breakfast – her rumbling stomach demanded that much. *A chef and she didn't even offer me breakfast,* Elle scoffed, pulling up to a breakfast and lunch spot full of businessmen and women having their first meal of the day.

. . .

Her phone vibrated: *Had a lot of fun last night tho,* the message read.

Tho? Elle shook her head, bashing herself for wasting her time this way. What was she trying to prove anyway? She hadn't moved on. She knew exactly who she wanted to see and it wasn't Louisa.

"What will it be, ma'am?" The barista looked at her bemused. She'd been standing in front of the wall menu for a couple of minutes.

"Uhm... A salmon bagel and black coffee, thanks."

She sat down with her order, eyeing the other customers. People watching had always been a nasty habit of hers, one indulgence she couldn't let go of, no matter how hard she tried. People in suits and dressed business casual lined up to get their everyday coffee, all dressed the same, all doing boring corporate jobs. She noticed one interruption to the queue's pattern; Kiera O'Malley's fiery red hair stood out from the sea of black and grey.

In need of some distraction from her problems, Elle waved her over.

"How's it going, what were you up to in this area?" Kiera asked, sitting down opposite to Elle.

"Pff, long story," Elle ran her hand through the tangle of her hair, still unbrushed. "What have you been up to?"

Kiera dug her fork into the rich caesar salad. "Oh, my grandmother lives nearby, I help her out sometimes on my free days."

Elle took the last bite of her bagel into her mouth and chewed, nodding. "Very good," she hummed.

"You look like a mess," Kiera smiled, "like a *morning after* mess."

. . .

Elle spread her arms out in surrender. "Solved the mystery, congrats."

"How was she?"

"Don't ask," Elle raised her eyes in a gloomy look, "it was a disaster. Not the sex, it was fine," she smirked, "just... I think I was looking for something else this time."

"What, did she try to trap you within a-" Kiera gasped theatrically, "monogamous relationship? Did she want you to propose?"

Elle shook her head, "that's not funny, Kiera."

"Oh... You were the one who wanted something serious?"

. . .

Elle nodded. "These days it's harder to get than I thought."

"How about that cute ER doctor you've been hanging around with every chance you get?"

"What, Maya?" Elle scoffed, "no she is a finished case. She doesn't want me. Not anymore, anyway. She's really just acting immature, is what she's doing," Elle said and immediately regretted her words. She wished she could pull them back into her mouth, but it was too late.

"Oh well, if that's what you think," Kiera nodded. "Dating is hard, man, I've been single for two years now."

"Why'd you break up, you and the person you'd been with before?" Elle became significantly interested in breakup stories as of late, as if to justify to herself her mistake.

. . .

"He turned out to be a douchebag, nothing very original. Cheated, abused alcohol, all that." Kiera shrugged, "I'm way past that now, he deserves to rot."

"But is cheating absolutely unforgivable, you think?" Elle leaned lower over the table.

"Probably depends on the situation. I think it can contribute to the general… profile of the person, how secure they make you feel, etc. I think it's more about breaking the other person's trust and lying, disrespecting their feelings, rather than the sex itself. Would you agree?" Kiera looked up from her salad to see Elle completely engrossed in her words. "Elle?"

"I don't know. I think… Love also has to include forgiveness," she said, getting up to give the tray back to the staff. "I'll probably be on my way, Kiera. Nice chat, but I need to finally shower."

. . .

"Yeah, I'm not hugging you goodbye then," Kiera laughed and they waved to each other.

Getting in her car, Elle resolved to try to get back with Maya by any means possible. There was no one else she'd want, until she was completely certain she'd done every single thing she could to get back her love. She'd continue writing in her journal, she'd try to understand what had led her to cheat, she would do everything in her power to feel Maya's skin against her own again.

8

MAYA

The blazing sun, like a thief, found its way inside the emergency room's office, leaking in through the gaps in between covered windows and see-through doors. Maya wiped her sweaty forehead, for the first time in weeks actively counting the time left until the end of her shift. Her fingers felt sticky inside the rubber gloves, and the number of patients was steadily increasing during the dense summer days. Elderly patients with heart or lung issues doubled each day.

Suddenly, disturbing the peace, Maya's pager flashed and vibrated. "Suspected heat stroke. Fallen elderly woman trapped in apartment. Other injuries possible. Dr. Monroe to attend the scene with Ambulance 13."

Maya grabbed her medical bag and made her way to the ambulance bay where she got on board with the crew.

"How did that even happen?" Maya asked, breaking the silence inside the car.

"Apparently, her grandson locked the house by habit, forgetting she was inside and taking the only pair of keys with him. Then the neighbors saw something was wrong with her through the kitchen window. Apparently, she fell."

"Shit." Maya sighed. She was hoping the lady hadn't hit anything on her way to the floor, especially not with her head – that would practically mean a death sentence.

When they got to the place, a team of firefighters was already looking for the flat. It was *the* team of firefighters, Maya realized, before following them upstairs.

Of course it was.

Elena Rodriguez was everywhere she went at the moment. A beautiful torture.

A dark jacket ahead of her spelled RODRIGUEZ. The staircase seemed to stretch into infinity, its dark corridor shone with the grease of a new layer of paint. The smell of it was intoxicating, making Maya's head spin. In the heat, every scent grew in intensity to an unbearable degree, their sweat mingled with the smell of paint. The lady lived on the sixth floor, and by the time they got there, everyone was struggling to catch their breath.

Having located the door, the firefighters began knocking it down. It was a heavy, sturdy thing, the kind installed in hotels and such to prevent burglars, or perhaps fires. Finally, it gave way.

Maya and the rest of her team stormed inside, finding the woman passed out on the floor wound full of blood decorated the right side of her forehead.

Maya moved quickly checking her pulse, weak but steady. She got some fluids attached to start rehydrating the woman, and the paramedics put the cooling blanket across her. These basics done, it would be best to get her on the ambulance and to the hospital.

They quickly got her onto the stretcher and the firefighters carried her down to the ambulance. One of the people handling her was Elle, but occupied with the rescue, Maya couldn't pay much attention to her.

They were professional who often worked with each other but that was it. Elle's beautiful green eyes looked troubled, but Maya tried to ignore them.

On the grounds next to the building, they began assessing the woman's state. The situation was much better than anyone had expected, and provided she got to the hospital quickly enough, her chances of survival seemed great. Everyone let out a little sigh of relief while getting the woman into the car with her oxygen mask on.

"I'll get back on my own," Maya shouted to the paramedics, knowing it was well past the end of her shift, and she let the ambulance leave without her.

She craved rest, somewhere quiet and cool. Whatever gentle breeze blew her way, she felt her sweaty body shiver. There was something familiar about this neighborhood, something telling her she'd been here before. The cobblestone pathways and tree-lined alleys led somewhere she was certain she would recognize.

Suddenly, a hand grabbed her shoulder, startling her.

"What--?" she turned around, standing face to

face with Elle. "Where's your crew?" She raised her eyebrow.

"Oh, I asked them to leave me. I was finishing my shift anyway. Where is your crew?"

Elle was on her own in her navy blue fire department shirt and pants. The muscles of her arms glowed a beautful bronze. Her dark hair was in a messy bun.

Uncharacteristic silence crept up between them. Elle got a bit closer, her eyes steadily laid on Maya's face, lowering a little to her lips. Maya didn't know where to look or what to do with her body. She felt a sense of peace after an exhausting effort, the waves of cool evening breeze relaxing her following the hot, bustling day. For a moment, she wanted to forget what had happened between her and Elle. She wanted to relax into her like a stranger, someone containing all the mysteries of their personality, or mistakes, still untouched.

When Elle closed the space between them, Maya allowed herself to lean into her body. She looked up, surprised to find the same sensation she'd felt all those years ago. She felt her body fit into Elle's perfectly, just like before, as if they'd never separated. Elle raised Maya's chin, and their lips met – this time gently, as if they wanted to lick out a confession from one another. Elle's lips felt soft and moist, like a pond of water against the day's draught. Maya drove her fingers up her neck, reaching for her hair to weave her fingers into. Whenever their eyes would meet, they'd look away. As if in a dance of shadows, their bodies clung to each other but their minds stayed conflicted. Maya moved down to Elle's neck. She laid a trail of kisses on her throat, then kissed her way back up again to Elle's lips, slipping her tongue in and trailing the inside of her mouth, slowly, deliberately. Their hips clashed, and Maya was certain she wouldn't walk away without having all of Elle. The need growing rapidly moist in between her thighs pushed any memory of their dispute into the furthest corners of her mind, bending its shape into that of physical desire. She wanted Elle, and the knowledge that she could have her made her drunk on the thought of it. She pulled Elle's hips closer and rapidly pushed her tongue inside Elle's mouth so as to make Elle quietly moan.

"We're in public." Elle pulled her away, flustered.

"So take me to yours," Maya said in a seductive

tone she hadn't used in a long time. "You live nearby, no?"

The quiet satisfaction of placing this neighborhood in her memory made Maya grin to herself. Elle smiled, putting her hands in her pockets. She was still wearing her uniform pants and a simple navy blue fire department shirt she usually wore beneath her jacket. The sight of Elle's toned arms and the outline of her breasts in that top made Maya want to carry her to the house.

"I do, I'm fifteen minutes away," Elle pointed out the direction.

They held hands while walking, and Maya thought of nothing besides her fast beating heart. Kissing Elle felt like breaking the rules. It felt forbidden, and all the more delicious. It felt intoxicating, like the little sips of whiskey you had hidden in a cupboard, like sneaking out back when they were teenagers. She said she didn't want to talk to Elle – but putting her tongue inside of her wasn't exactly *talking*, was it? Making her moan wasn't a *conversation*, either. Maybe sex fitted within what she could permit herself. A familiar gravel path crunched beneath their feet, and Maya knew they were close.

She hoped Elle wouldn't try to talk to her.

Their words always came out tangled, creating complicated knots. No, Maya was craving something naked and raw, something she had felt hidden in Elle's mouth and waiting to be tasted again.

"Here we are," Elle smoothly opened the door.

"You live alone?"

"Mhmm."

There were a million things going through Maya's head as she stepped into the beautiful house, but she said none of them. She didn't comment on the tastefully high ceilings, the size of the house, the collection of expensive paintings. This house stood as proof to her that time passes for everyone, that not only she, but Elle, had also undergone a string of changes and successes of which Maya would never know the full scope.

Unimportant, she thought, pinning Elle to the wall.

I'm just here for one thing.

She teased Elle's lips with her tongue mercilessly, licking them gently then pulling away whenever Elle opened her mouth to pursue a kiss. Maya saw her gasp with blissful annoyance, saw her legs twitch, and her body, maybe even a part of her mind, felt at home.

She put her hands beneath the fabric of Elle's shirt, climbing up the familiar, muscled stomach, up to the soft skin of her breasts in a crop top, so softly feminine and contrasting with the steel firmness of the rest of her body. She thought it a delicious privilege to be able to access such a sensitive part of Elle, hidden away and protected. Maya took her time to feel the hardening nipples beneath her fingers, making Elle quietly moan – a sound she'd learned to forget craving at night, but which now would surely come back to her each evening. She could smell the familiar scent of Elle's sweat mingling with that sweet smokiness that lingered in her hair that Maya had always enjoyed.

"Should we see your bedroom?" she whispered directly into Elle's ear, knowing how quickly the shivers would travel down her spine.

Elle nodded, flustered. Walking up the staircase, Maya wondered whether any other girl made her flustered this way, or whether it had stayed the same, whether the only person to really know this side of Elle remained Maya.

They entered the bedroom absorbed in their kiss, their limbs reaching for each other like drowning women looking for something to save them. They kept seeking each other's faces as if they were sunflowers at the early hours of dawn, looking for something nourishing, looking for their source of life. Maya's mind sat back in a momentary truce, crossed its arms and put a blindfold on, letting her body do what it had to do. Her senses took the reins, guiding her hands to pull the shirt and crop top off Elle's body, to inhale the earthy scent of her skin and lick her way up from her abdomen back to her mouth.

"Did you miss me?" Elle asked, half sighing from anticipation. Her hand ran through Maya's hair to finally rest on the back of her neck.

Maya froze for a second. "Don't talk," She looked up at Elle from between her breasts, her eyes sparkling.

"..All right." Elle flashed a mischievous smile, one that said *I know what you're doing.*

Elle knew what Maya needed and was prepared to go along with it.

Thank god for that.

Maya knew she couldn't stop her body now from taking what it so badly needed, even if she'd wanted to. Something about Elle was like a drug to her. Maya could barely remember any sex she'd had since Elle. Nothing that had lit her whole body as on fire as it was now.

Maya pulled her own shirt off, then Elle's pants and underwear followed suit. She knew how turned on Elle got from being the only one entirely naked, and she took full advantage of that, running her hands up Elle's thighs and circling around her pussy. Then she went up her back, touching her skin up to her neck, and went back down again, fondling her ass. She had missed this for sure, seeing Elle stand naked for her, showing off her beautiful body and waiting to see what Maya did with it. Elle shivered at her every touch. Elle's eyes had submitted willingly to her. She was giving it all up for her, and she liked it.

"I can't wait to see you come for me," Maya said. She couldn't wait, and her fingers teased for a moment or two before sliding them inside Elle. "Just look at you, so wet and ready for me." She wasn't supposed to talk, but couldn't stop herself. It felt too good to be back. It felt too good to be the smug one.

Elle nodded, and that on its own made Maya shiver. She took Elle to the bed, and Elle knowingly sat down on its edge, spreading her legs. Maya patted her thigh.

"You remember everything, don't you," she

whispered, seeing how Elle was following exactly the way Maya liked to fuck her.

She knelt in front of her, devouring her wet and wanting pussy. Maya had forgotten how good it tasted. She wanted to lose herself down here forever. Forget everything else. The taste of Elle's pleasure on her tongue gave her everything she wanted. Elle moaned loudly. Every movement of her tongue left Elle pushing further into her face trying to get a better pressure for herself. Maya licked and sucked, enjoying what she had missed so much for so long. She stopped for a moment, gesturing to the bed.

"I want you to sit on my face," she purred, laying down and waving Elle over.

Elle obediently made her way up the bed, moving to kneel above Maya's face. Their eyes met for a second just before Maya pulled Elle down onto her waiting mouth. Maya felt the kind of hunger born out of satiation—the more she had of Elle's body, the more she craved, in a gluttonous madness fueled by their disagreements, the tension, the longing boiling just below both of their skins. She kept licking and sucking, enjoying Elle's moans. She pulled Elle down so her pussy was tight to her face just how she liked it. She was trying to persuade Elle to grind down on her face and to ride her with abandon like she used to, and it took a couple of minutes of eager licking and pulling down on Elle's thighs before Elle gave into her own desires, closed her eyes, held on tight to the headboard and began to grind deep and slow against Maya's face. Maya relaxed herself into it until she felt Elle's thighs shiver, and her moans get louder. She knew she was close. But Maya had no desire to let her go so fast. She was planning on drawing it out the longest she could. She wanted Elle begging for it, begging and crying. Maya pushed her thighs upward, taking her mouth away.

"Come on, Maya." Elle sighed, her eyes half-closed.

Maya only held her ass firmer and tortured her further. Elle began trying to help herself grinding her hips again, but it didn't help much. Maya was clearly in charge of her body and wasn't going to let that go so quickly. She wanted Elle begging, and nothing else would do.

"Maya, please," Elle moaned, then moaned something completely unintelligible, both of which Maya took with pleasure.

Maya teased with her tongue, drawing it back

and forth lightly, her hands forbidding Elle from lowering herself and grinding on Maya's face in the way that they both knew she so desperately needed.

"Beg me. If you want it, Elena. I want you to look me in the eyes and beg me for exactly what you want."

Elle's eyes opened slowly, and her gaze met Maya's. There were a few seconds where Maya just looked up at her from between her legs before Elle began to speak, her voice hesitant and laced with a sweet desperation.

"Please... Maya. I... I need to come." Elle's green eyes were earnest. "I need to grind on your face until I come. I need to come in your sweet mouth. Please."

Maya waited just a second longer before she nodded. "Okay, Baby." She pulled Elle back down until her pussy was tight against her face. Maya knew this was Elle's favorite thing ever. The one thing that would always tip her over the edge. Clearly it was still the case.

Elle began to grind down against Maya's face and Maya dove back in with her mouth with enthusiasm.

Maya could barely breathe, but she didn't care. All she could see, smell, taste was her.

Elle.

She gripped her thighs and held on tightly as Elle took her pleasure. Her grinding became deeper, and her moans became louder. Her breathing quickened, and she came loud and hard, gushing in Maya's mouth.

Maya swallowed eagerly, breathing Elle in, taking everything from her. Elle's body sat high above her, bronzed muscled glistening in sweat.

She is so fucking beautiful.

Maya released her slowly and watched as Elle collapsed forward against the headboard before falling down onto the bed, breathing heavily. Elle lay on her back, gathering herself up. Maya approached, placing her hand between her still-shivering thighs, menacing.

"I'm all sensitive now." Elle sighed. "What are you doing?"

"You're not sensitive on the inside though, are you?" Maya grinned, one thing on her mind.

Elle raised her eyebrows, comprehending. She pointed to the first drawer of the nightstand next to her bed and slowly raised herself up to be on all fours. Memories flooded back to Maya. The sight made Maya gulp, and before she went to fetch what was needed, she went up to gently lick the trail up Elle's pussy and over her asshole, making her dip her back further, raising her ass in that heavenly way to expose herself fully. Maya wanted nothing more than to pound the living hell out of her.

She kissed her ass cheek, saying "I'll be back in a second," then patted her ass and was on the way to the nightstand.

Upon opening the drawer, she smiled widely.

"Do you wanna scream, or do you wanna scream?" She admired the collection of dildos varied in shapes and sizes, already setting her mind on one. Putting the leather harness on, she turned back to Elle, "Hm?"

"I'll take whatever you choose," Elle tried sounding nonchalant, but her voice was coated heavily with the feeling of her heartbeat.

Maya finished getting herself ready, and came back up to Elle, dragging her to the edge of the bed.

"Come on, raise that ass higher," she said, putting a few fingers in Elle's pussy to study how wet it still was. "Oh, we don't need lubricant," she whispered. "Elle, spit on it."

Elle turned around, obediently spitting on the dildo, at the same time blushing at its size.

"Come on, it was in your drawer, don't act surprised," Maya scoffed. She put her fingers back inside, circling around slowly, warming Elle up.

"Yeah, I don't usually…use them on myself…"

"You mean you don't get fucked the way I fuck you?" Maya ran her other hand through Elle's hair. "Poor darling, but you like it so much." She put the cold tip of the dildo against her opening, making Elle quietly gasp.

"I only like it when you do it," Elle admitted. "Doesn't feel right with others."

"I love to hear that." Maya twisted Elle's hair in her hand and pulled her head up, bending her back to its maximum. "Take it for me well," she said before thrusting roughly into her.

It didn't take her a long time to begin mercilessly pounding Elle with all her strength. Her body quickly remembered its way, and the rhythm drew the best out of Elle. She began moaning within a minute, the high-pitched, delicate moans Maya had a weakness for.

She might be a big tough firefighter, but that just made it all the sweeter for Maya to take her like this.

"I missed your moaning," she said, panting.

"Fuck me harder, please," Elle managed to fit in between one gasp for air and another.

"No problem," Maya took Elle's hips in her hands and slammed herself into Elle as if it were the last time she'd ever fuck.

The delicate moaning turned into long, loud screaming. Maya dug her fingers into Elle's thighs as she slammed relentlessly into her, desperate to make her come a second time, confident she was hitting just the right spot. The melody she got out of Elle while getting deep into her pussy was something she enjoyed beyond measure. Suddenly, she slowed down the thrusts, looking to hear Elle's meek begging for more.

She didn't disappoint. Elle twisted her head and sweetly moaned to get it harder.

"Please.. Maya... fuck me.." Maya relished in the sight, feeling her own wetness drip onto the dildo and harness. Maya rewarded her by thrusting into her again and again building her rhythm once again.

"I want you to come for me like a good little slut, Elena. You'll come when I say so."

Elle was moaning and incoherent. Maya had never known anyone enjoy rough fucking like Elle did, and it was the sweetest pleasure to give it to her.

Maya reached her right hand under Elle's hip. "I'm going to touch your clit for you wile I fuck you and you are going to come hard for me, okay?"

Maya slid her fingers against Elle's clitoris as she kept fucking her faster and faster. "Come for me, Elena. Come for my big dick."

Elle exploded beneath her, shuddering, screaming, shaking. Maya smiled to herself. She still had it. She pulled out slowly, allowing Elle to collapse prone onto the bed.

Maya got out of the harness and walked around the bed, raising Elle's dizzy-with-pleasure head up to meet her eyes.

"I want you to feel something," she took Elle's hand and drove it down to her own dripping wet, untouched vulva. She left her hand there, letting Elle feel the entirety of her.

"I guess the party's not over yet," Elle said, coming back to life, spreading Maya's legs wide apart and taking her place between her thighs. Maya put her hand on Elle's head, guiding her however she liked.

She had to admit, Elle's tongue felt the best. Quickly, her mind floated away, or rather dissipated into her body. There was nothing left but her body's intense pleasure driving her to the edge of perception. She gripped Elle's hair tighter, expecting her to finish her off.

Instead, Elle pulled away, only torturing her further with her fingers, leaving Maya in quiet spasms of craving.

"I want you to come on my face," she murmured, lying down.

Maya had no choice but to follow or go mad with this bodily craving. Elle's touch was the only thing she cared for at the moment, so she knelt obediently above Elle's face, spreading her legs wide. She felt a slap on her ass and looked at Elle in complete surprise.

"Look at you, what a good girl," Elle said before diving back in to finish what she'd started.

The words tightened Maya's chest in a long-forgotten wave of pleasure. Her cheeks reddened as she gave into the feeling of intense abandon within her body and felt her climax rush over her like a lightning bolt, electrifying her body and leaving her gasping for air.

They lay down, completely exhausted. Their breathing grew deeper and calmer, and with time, they fell asleep lying side by side atop the still neatly tucked-in bedsheets.

It was a quarter to six a.m. when Maya woke up. She moved away from Elle, startled, the memories of the night quickly coming back to her. Elle was still tightly held by sleep, her breath rhythmically making her bare chest rise and fall, and Maya couldn't help but admire for a moment Elle's naked body, so deeply undisturbed and peaceful.

Soon, she realized she'd rather leave without waking her up. She got dressed in a hurry, then in a few moments was out of the house, thinking of how stupid it had been to leave her clothes at the hospital. She had to pass the neighborhood of neat lawns and white houses in her ER medic's uniform.

The sun was up, but it was the unmistakably cold morning sun, and after a while of walking, she began shivering. Finally, she reached a bus station. Having studied the infinitely complicated map of the station, she directed her steps toward the bus that would take her home.

On the bus, she could no longer escape the

flood of thoughts connected to her night with Elle. The lame dam she'd set up during the hookup burst unceremoniously, and she realized what a mess she'd gotten them both into.

No, we both did that.

She nodded, reassuring herself. The fault lay on both sides.

Little rivers of regret began forming in her mind, she chastised herself for leaving without a note or a goodbye kiss. But then, she didn't really feel in the mood for a goodbye kiss. Something kept telling her that for Elle, it was just another hookup, just to prove to herself she could still pull Maya.

But it wasn't that, was it? she smiled.

No, she knew there was something special about it. She could see that Elle would never have this kind of sex with anyone else. Did this mean they still meant something special to each other? Would Maya want that to be the case?

Oh, stop it, silly. It's only sex.

She shook her head, putting her earphones in and dozing off to her favorite 70's playlist.

Of course, she'd miss her stop.

9

ELLE

Elle woke up with her head in a tangle from the avalanche of dreams that had haunted her the whole night after sleeping with Maya. When she realized she was alone, she buried her head in her hands, sitting this way for what felt like hours.

She had to gather herself up before her shift started, and the two hours, she knew, would pass cruelly quickly.

"What the fuck have I done," she muttered to herself, getting dressed.

She was certain that now Maya would see her as the fuckgirl she already thought her. The way she'd simply left while Elle was still asleep burnt a hole in her chest, made her feel like an old couch on which people don't hesitate to extinguish their cigarettes. She wanted to simultaneously apologize and ask for an apology. She wanted to feel Maya's lips on hers again and yet never see her again all at once.

Driving to work, she resolved to reach out. She had no idea about Maya's shifts and was silently hoping that the reason for her departure on the sly was work and not unfavorable feelings toward Elle.

After a while, she also began chastising herself for getting so vulnerable with Maya, particularly sexually. It was like opening a part of herself she'd kept hidden, safely tucked away, on their first night together. She grew afraid Maya would think nothing of it—discard it as something simple, like a preference. But it clearly wasn't just a preference. It was something showing Elle's complete openness with her. Elle didn't have sex like that with other women, that was for sure.

She got home, exhausted from her shift. Elle's crew had been called to assist another station with a barn fire, and even though the building was devoid of any inhabitants, it was hell to extinguish. Rural fires were hard work. All fetching and carrying heavy pumps and hoses because there never seemed to be a super convenient water source once you got far from the city.

She cast her bag right next to the front door and dialed Maya's number, biting her nails while waiting on the line.

"Yes?"

Elle's breath got shallower at hearing Maya's voice. It sounded tired, dry. Elle began pacing the room, picking out the best words she could find.

"Hey, I wanted to talk. If you're free, of course."

She heard Maya sigh and thought the sound betrayed something close to bitterness, but she chalked it up to work-related exhaustion.

"You could stop by around noon tomorrow, if it's your free day. I'm taking the day off," Maya finally suggested.

"It's my free day, I just finished my shift." Elle smiled.

"Great. See you then." Maya quickly hung up.

Elle stood in the middle of her living room, feeling quite upset by Maya's tone. She didn't know how much more strength this whole situation would require of her, but she felt determined to set it right.

The evening was approaching quickly, and with it the group bar outing Elle had promised her team to attend. She showered, put on a lazy, all-black outfit—black jeans and a simple black T-shirt—and tied up her hair in a neat high ponytail. She felt as ready to go as she could, given that she was in no mood for partying.

Awaiting her were almost all her friends besides Kaia Montgomery, who'd landed a shift the same evening.

"It's Rory's turn to buy the drinks." Haley welcomed Elle with a quick embrace and cast a glance at Rory.

"Well, whatever you say, baby," Rory responded, getting up.

Having received their drinks, everyone loosened up a little, digging their heads out of their individual problems and dilemmas. At the end of the day, the group was Elle's respite and family, and she couldn't help smiling the whole evening.

The next round of drinks was on her, however, and that brought her mood slightly down.

Emboldened by alcohol, they entered the stage of confessions, each bringing to the table something that weighed heavy on their hearts.

"I royally fucked it up, girls," Elle pressed her forehead to the table in resignation.

"What happened?" Kiera patted her back with a tipsy kind of motion. "I'm sure it's not that bad."

"I slept with my ex." Elle looked around her friend' faces, "and she's mad at me now, I think."

They laughed, wanting to cheer her up.

"It can't be that bad if she slept with you." Haley added, "Do you wanna get back together?"

Elle realized what a mistake it had been to try and share the situation in such a spontaneous way. Its intricacies tied around her throat, and she wished she'd never spoken about it.

"It's complicated. I did something bad when we were together before, but no matter. I'm seeing her tomorrow. Wish me luck," and with that, she took a massive gulp of her whiskey.

"Cheers to that." The group clinked their glasses.

Elle stood at Maya's front door the following day, wishing she hadn't had so much whiskey the night before, Elle had no idea where the conversation would take them, but she was willing to simply plunge into it and see for herself. Partially, she felt like a little kid waiting to be admitted to the principal's office. Another part of her wanted to play it cool, remain nonchalant and confident. But she knew it was no use trying to pretend around Maya. Finally, she rang the bell.

The staircase felt somewhat familiar, and she wondered why that would be. This place had surely never belonged to Maya or her family. On the third floor, she bravely knocked.

"You don't have to knock," Maya swiftly opened the door. "There is a doorbell here, too."

"Don't be so rude." Elle shook her head, walking into the flat.

"Sorry."

"Whose flat is this? I somehow remember it but can't place from where." Elle looked around, glad of this opportunity to chit chat. "It's empty as hell, though. Where is all your stuff?"

"I think you've been here before because this used to be Magdalena's flat. Her parents use it as an Airbnb now. I'm moving soon to my own apartment, so this is only temporary."

"Oh, nice." Elle sat down on the couch.

"Would you like some coffee?" Maya offered coldly.

"Sure." Elle put her hands on her knees, something she always did when uncomfortable.

Maya disappeared into the kitchen without another word. Elle felt a bit foolish, confronted with such a wall of ice after the intense night. She got up and followed her, leaning against the kitchen counter.

Maya looked so beautiful, her golden hair loose around her shoulders, but she was angry, that much was clear.

"Why so distant?" she asked simply.

Maya turned around to face her, leaning against the opposite counter.

"I don't know what it is that you want to have with me." She avoided Elle's eyes. "But I don't like it."

"What don't you like?" Elle raised her eyebrows in shock. "I only want to be with you, Maya. Didn't you see how vulnerable I became in there with you? I don't have sex like that with anyone else. All I'm doing is trying to get back together with you! Yeah, you were right back there when we were against the ambulance. I just didn't have the guts to say--"

"Don't bullshit me," Maya snapped.

"What?" Elle felt extremely confused on top of being hurt.

"Don't bullshit me. I found your little dating profile on Her App." She paused for a moment, gathering words. "If all you want with me is some casual fun on the side while you're out there while you're looking for someone to actually date--"

"Stop this." Elle grew furious, hearing Maya's interpretation of her actions. *Such a distorted, inaccurate pile of bullshit.* She tried to tame her emotions but fell short. "Don't you see how much I care about you? That was nothing, some bullshit experimenting that means nothing to me. I forgot about that goddamned profile. I want you!" She leaned in closer, looking into Maya's hesitant eyes. "I really do. I don't feel right with anyone else."

"I don't believe you."

"What?" Being so close to Maya's face, her dark brown eyes flashing dangerously, Elle could barely separate the meaning of her words from the heat of her breath she could feel on her skin, from the movement of her dark red lips. "You're wearing lipstick." Elle smiled, shamelessly stroking Maya's lower lip with her thumb.

Maya stood frozen, taken by surprise with this

turn of events. "I am," she said, barely moving her lips so as not to disturb Elle's finger.

Elle put her hand on Maya's back to pull her closer. "Was it for me?"

"Yes." Maya nodded, hesitantly putting her tongue out and licking the length of Elle's thumb, taking it in her mouth.

Elle shivered at the feel of Maya's tongue.

"Oh, Baby, you look so very beautiful." Elle lifted her to sit on the countertop, putting her hips against Maya's.

Elle drove her hand up Maya's thigh, beneath the fabric of her skirt. Her fingers stroked the lace underwear she found between her thighs, whispering, "It feels so good against my fingers."

Maya shivered, pulling Elle closer to renew their kiss. Their connection was so strong and instinctive. Elle followed Maya's cue, still playing around with Maya's underwear, tangling it in her fingers, teasing at Maya's vulva underneath.

"Should I take you like this, on the countertop?" she teased.

Maya eluded the question, kissing her more intensely.

"Oh, you want to be taken on the countertop." Elle smirked, pushing two fingers past the now damp fabric into Maya's wet pussy, hearing her sigh in her quiet, involuntary way. She delighted in feeling Maya grow increasingly wet around her fingers in anticipation. "Let's take it off," Elle removed her fingers and helped Maya to remove the lace underwear.

Once the underwear was gone, Elle parted Maya's thighs and dipped her head, licking at Maya's pussy. She felt the tickle of Maya's neat, perfect pubic hair. She tasted Maya's arousal and enjoyed Maya's moans as they increased.

She sucked at Maya's clitoris. Maya gasped and grabbed a handful of her hair.

"Oh my god," Maya said, and Elle increased her assault on Maya's pussy with her mouth.

She moved her right hand to assist her in her quest and pushed two strong fingers back inside Maya, curling them upward to find Maya's G-spot.

"Oh fuck, Elena. Please…" Maya was coming apart for her, and Elle couldn't think of anything she enjoyed more. Her name on Maya's lips as she fucked her was an absolute pleasure.

Elle went to work with her fingers, fucking Maya with them hard and fast as her mouth licked and sucked Maya's clitoris.

It wasn't long before Maya's moans became

screams and Elle felt her tighten around her fingers and squirt as she came.

Elle smiled to herself as she slowly withdrew her fingers and emerged from under Maya's skirt. Her own desire throbbed insistently between her legs.

She met Maya's dark brown eyes that were now glazed with lust. Maya was clearly in a post orgasmic haze. Elle needed to take her own pleasure so desperately. She could feel her own wetness between her legs.

"Can I, Baby?" Elle growled.

Maya knew what she was asking and nodded, offering her arms. "Help me down?" Maya asked, barely able to speak.

Elle helped her down onto the kitchen floor until Maya was kneeling, looking adoringly up at her from the cool tiles.

Elle quickly dropped her own pants and underwear to the floor and straddled Maya's face in a standing position.

"Let me use your face, baby. Let me come in your mouth," Elle murmured as Maya began to lick.

Elle grabbed the back of Maya's golden hair and tangled it in her fingers. She drew Maya's beautiful face tight to her pussy and thrust her hips so she could grind herself on Maya's face.

That was how she liked it the most. Grinding on her, taking her pleasure on Maya's face. Maya was merely passive beneath her. It didn't really matter if she was licking or not. Looking down at Maya's beautiful face between her legs and feeling that pressure against her clitoris was enough.

Seconds later, Elle exploded, coming loud and hard on Maya's face, gushing into Maya's mouth. Maya desperately swallowed, determined to take Elle's orgasm in her mouth.

"Fuck, Babe, that was so good," Elle said as she slowly released her grip on Maya's head and looked down at Maya licking her lips, the wetness of Elle's climax still evident all over her face.

Fuck, she looks so hot.

Elle sat down on the floor next to her and drew Maya into her arms. Elle whispered in her ear, "Don't leave me alone like that again. That was really rude."

"Okay." Maya turned to her. "I think you should go, though. I have a meeting soon. I forgot to tell you."

"You *forgot to tell me*? Maya don't do this to me.

What is this?" Elle got up, "We didn't even talk anything through."

"Since when are you the one who wants to talk things through?" Maya sat up, raising an eyebrow in suspicion.

"Since I've started to journal," Elle said in a flat tone which made Maya laugh.

"You journal?"

"Don't make me feel silly about it," Elle protested, picking up her shirt. "You were always the one telling me to work on my emotions, so I'm doing that now."

"Well, I'm sorry for laughing," Maya said in a more serious tone. "It's good, you're right. I really meant it about the meeting, though. It's with Arthur, my real estate agent."

"Yeah, well, what can I say to *Arthur the real estate agent?*" Elle mocked, this time making Maya laugh on purpose.

At the door, she gave Elle a quick kiss, and Elle could taste her own climax on Maya's lips. "Don't make me care about you so much," she said, closing the door.

What the fuck Elle thought the whole three floors on the stairs, then the entire way home. She felt cheerful, but also extremely confused. She liked that Maya was open to her again, and that their sexual chemistry was very much intact, but her last remark had caught Elle completely off guard. She hoped she could catch Captain Ramirez on her next shift and talk to someone with more life experience, because this whole Maya thing was proving too difficult for her to handle.

While driving, she felt her phone vibrate – a text message. She couldn't check it while driving. she'd seen and been called to too many car accidents caused by texting and driving. So for the remainder of the way she sat as if on needles, praying for it to be a message from Maya. Her mind ran as far as guessing the contents of the hypothetical message, its tone, whether it would mean another meeting, etc.

Finally reaching her destination and parking the car, she took the phone out of her pocket and nervously unlocked the screen. For a few seconds she simply sat there looking at it hopelessly, realizing how stupid it had been to get so excited. The text message was from Louisa, who Elle had almost completely forgotten existed.

Elle blocked the phone number, feeling utterly evil, then got out of the car and went inside her apartment, dragging her feet as if they were made of lead, wishing to at least find one bottle of whiskey tucked away somewhere in a far corner of her fridge.

Obviously, the day no longer a bit of luck in store for her. She found no trace of whiskey or any other alcohol around her apartment, so she sat sober on the couch. She took up her journal, ready to diligently describe her emotional state. Journaling was beginning to be favorite hobby.

10

MAYA

The still-packed carton boxes daunted Maya each time she entered her newly-inhabited apartment. Usually, she would come in exhausted from work with only a big dinner on her mind as well as sleep. Deep, restorative sleep.

On the night following her day off, she finally decided to begin unpacking the nightmare cartons populating her living room. As soon as she started, the activity completely immersed her. Sitting on the floor and grouping her various belongings together, she found completely forgotten clothes, paintings that used to decorate her bedroom walls, and books. She liked seeing them fit into neatly assigned groups. It gave her a sense of security.

She still had no furniture besides the bed and her kitchen. Everything she owned lay around the too-clean floor. Doing all this with no help was a tiring pursuit. Moving into a new house seemed to her to be an activity one would do while in love, joking around and arguing about minuscule things such as the color of the carpet or the height of the kitchen counter.

Having sorted almost all the boxes, Maya realized she'd been unpacking them for almost four hours, and the night had already spread its wings over the city. She yawned. Thinking about getting ready for her early shift tomorrow with five hours of sleep in her made her want to lie down and never wake up from the blissful, dreamful state.

She rose. Her bones stung with the consequences of sitting in one place for too long. Her back ached to be stretched, but her mind was only set on showering and making her head meet her pillow.

Standing in front of the mirror brushing her teeth, she suddenly felt a strong jolt. All her cups and bottles of soap fell in a rumbling chaos on the floor tiles. She instinctively held on to the sink, confused, clutching its edges with her toothbrush still hanging from her mouth.

She barely managed to set it on the sink and rinse her mouth when a wave of trembling shook her house, making her fall to her knees. The glass pane of the shower cabin shook dangerously, inches away from breaking, but not quite breaking just yet. The toothbrush and all other cosmetics that up until this moment had been tucked somewhere away, still keeping their place, finally fell to the ground. She thought of all the cautionary videos her teachers had showed her class, people hiding under their tables and waiting for the earthquake to be over. There wasn't a single table for her to hide under, and the shaking was still violently tugging on her apartment. She thought it must'd been at least a minute, which meant the earthquake would have wreaked havoc upon the city.

It quite simply meant disaster.

Once the shaking stopped, Maya weakly stood up, holding onto the sink. The wall mirror remained intact, as well as the glass shower pane, and she began deepening her breaths. The building had been recently constructed recently and apparently could withstand plenty. Maya grabbed her phone, going out to look whether everyone in the adjacent apartments had had as much luck as her. Knocking door to door, she encountered faces in shock and loud with gratefulness, people pulled their children close to their chests and prayed to whatever god had a hand in their safety.

Back in the disheveled apartment, Maya's phone exploded with messages from worried friends and family, but before she had time to respond to anyone, she received a call from her hospital.

"Dr. Monroe, are you safe and well?"

"Yes," Maya responded, her mind slowly catching up with the gravity of the situation.

"We need all our ER teams up and ready in the face of this sudden emergency. A large number of citizens have been trapped under collapsed buildings and other structures, we predict many rescue operations in the days to come."

"I'll be there within the hour." Maya glanced at the clock. It was 4:34 a.m. She shook herself out of self-pity. There were people whose life might depend on her professionalism and readiness.

Driving through the city, Maya felt as if she'd stepped into a different world. Even at the raw hour of dawn, chaos was already unfurling all around. Extravagant, one-family houses along the road had simply fallen to the ground, seemingly crumbling on their foundations. The wooden panels had broken to pieces like elongated dead hands sent chills down Maya's spine. The thought of families potentially stuck within their indented walls made her speed up toward the hospital. Her hands on the wheel felt as steady as during surgery, when the cold-minded focus would take over any of her emotions and lead her body, ingrained by years of training movement. She experienced a laser-sharp kind of focus, and the words *calm in the eye of the storm* bounced around her mind. Emotions would come before and after, but during the crucial moments, she had to be a machine. She had to let her hands lead her to believe she could save lives and remain impartial at the same time.

Driving through the neighborhoods full to the brim with housing complexes, she watched human tragedy unravel from the safety of her driver's seat. People stricken with ugly, animalistic fear, or hideously face-twisting grief. She had to keep herself in check – four a.m. thoughts have the crawling, overreaching quality that spreads about one's mind like slime, and even though Maya's body remained alert, her thoughts swam through ponds of muddy imaginations. Grief and pain could make even the most innocent faces resemble something terrifying, but as a doctor, she wasn't supposed to be thinking about that.

Police cars and fire trucks seemed so tightly knit to each other that they resembled strings of pearls pushing through the cracked open roads. Men and women in uniforms had so much work on their hands that they seemed lost. To Maya, they appeared to be so weighed down by the scope of their responsibilities that their steps became heavier than usual, their shoulders a few inches more slouched. Something sinister lay in the image of cars associated with emergency populating every corner of the city.

The sky, stretching out its last minutes of dawn, rolled out heavy clouds, only fittingly ominous, prophesying rain. Maya's throat felt dry and raspy, her head pulsing with the fire of a sleepless night and a taste of catastrophe.

~

Maya had never before seen the hospital so crowded, seemingly on the brim of bursting. She imagined the walls pulse and bend, almost like a living tissue, trying to accommodate the amount of victims from the earthquake.

The bustling noise unsettled her, its intensity carrying a form of unison. While the ER room was usually full of cries, pain, and anxiety, now it seemed like a new kind of experience altogether. These people were suffering for the same reason, their pain like invisible strings tying them all together. Maya set her bag aside and changed into hospital wear.

Busy discussing the way they'd dispatch the ambulances, Maya caught a glimpse of a policewoman being carried in.

"Hit by debris," her colleague clarified on the side.

A feeling she hadn't felt up to this point tied a thick, tight knot in the pit of her stomach, an emotion she reluctantly identified as dense fear. She knew her family was safe. Their building had withstood much worse, its sturdy architecture keeping them safe. And she'd received all of their worried-to-death-for-her messages. She couldn't know whether Elle was safe, as she'd probably be on duty rushing into the carnage, and that was what scared her. The awareness of Elle existing in the same city where the same massive earthquake had happened and caused so much death made Maya feel sick. The complete helplessness of not knowing whether Elle was safe at this exact moment washed over her like an ice-cold wave of anxiety.

I love her.

The team finally got inside the ambulance, driving out to the most affected sphere where most of their hospital's crew had been sent. They'd work closely with the firefighters to retrieve people from fallen buildings, most of them from their own homes.

"What a terrible fate," Maya said out loud, directing it more at the space ahead of her rather than any crew member in particular, "to be buried within your own home..."

They grimly nodded, and the driver sped up, feeling the same grasp of tragedy on his back.

11

ELLE

The second hour of the area assessment was nearing its end, and they still couldn't agree on how to retrieve the victims or conduct the search the most effectively. Elle, wildly out of her depth, could not offer anything besides following the operation plan once it was settled upon. Ramirez, Hunter, and Thompson had been discussing the matter with various technicians and emergency workers, seemingly without much progress.

The situation was looking grim, and all the firefighters seemed to catch reflections of their thoughts in each other's faces, worn-out and haunted by lack of sleep and an abundance of witnessed destruction.

It almost seemed inappropriate to Elle, the way the day simply continued on its path as if nothing had happened. The clouds rolled above their heads, but the sun had awakened, too, making them a bright and angelic color. The birds had begun their hunt, flying around in broad, peaceful circles. Everything in nature seemed to Elle so undisturbed, as if the disaster itself had not come strictly from nature. There were people barely holding onto their lives beneath the debris of buildings, and the captains couldn't agree on a safe way to retrieve them. Elle's eyes felt swollen and sore, needle-poked by the day's light. Not many firefighters were talking. The general ambience of grief took over their conversations.

"We know what we'll do." Thompson turned around to inform the team. "Twenty minutes and we'll be getting ready for the extrication."

The search dogs began barking, contributing to the bleak atmosphere. Kaia Montgomery stepped forward. "Is it a...rescue or ...recovery?" she asked Hallie Hunter in a quiet tone and Elle overheard.

"Rescue, as far as we know. There's a significant void within the collapsed building that we believe to contain living persons," Hunter explained, and there was an intimate moment between the two of them.

So they'd go in. It would be high risk, Elle understood. The ambulances showed up one by one, readying themselves to support the firefighters and receive the victims. The medical teams emerged onto the parking space. Elle ran her eyes along the crowd, scanning each face and unconsciously holding her breath. She needed to know if Maya was okay. Her nails bit into the skin of her palms, deeper, deeper, deeper...

There she was. Maya's golden head showed for a second above her colleague's arm. Was it her for certain? Elle kept on looking, holding in the rising panic in her chest. But no, Maya emerged out of the crowd, standing now at the front, in her green field medic uniform awaiting instructions. Her dark brown eyes were earnest. For a moment, Elle existed only by looking at Maya's silhouette against the backdrop of all the other medics, and that was her heartbeat, her breath, her thought.

Soon, however, Maya noticed her. Their gaze met, and even though they stood far from one another, they could clearly see each other – both of them stood frozen, overwhelmed with relief and some faint sense of realization. Mainly relief.

Shock and disbelief. Elle's breathing refused to remain easy. Her arms began trembling, her chest somehow grew tighter. Before she knew it, her vision was blurred by the tears cascading down her cheeks.

Maya moved from the place where she'd been standing. She ran, and Elle had no idea what to do, so she just stood in the same spot, watching as Maya separated from her group and jogged toward her.

Their embrace was as quick as lightning and equally invigorating. Elle didn't know how, but suddenly she was holding Maya's warm, alive – *alive!* – body in her arms, tightening them around her. Maya placed a hand against the back of her head and pull her in close.

"We'll get through this." Maya's voice reached her ears in a whisper, and then Maya was gone again, back with her crew.

They'd work until exhaustion hit. They'd work side by side, the whispered *we'll get through this* like a silent promise tying their efforts together, erasing whatever scars lay between them for the time of this crisis, bridging them like two bright cities against a black river of danger.

It was time for Elle to go into the rubble

accompanied by other emergency workers and the search dogs trained to find buried people. The engineers and commanders would stand in the established rescue base just around the corner, monitoring the rescue and guiding the team. Elle focused on her breathing, which was getting too shallow all too easily, betraying her feelings. This was the biggest disaster she'd ever witnessed, and going into a collapsed building wasn't something she was used to, although part of being a firefighter was expecting the unexpected.

Elle was one of the best at her job, and she couldn't let personal concerns about Maya cloud her professional judgement.

They began lifting the rubble from one layer of the building, sending in cameras and digging deeper into the ruin, dogs sniffing and carefully walking around. The familiar sensation of deep focus came over Elle's mind, and only the sounds of their various devices and the loud beating of her own heart remained, swimming in the now quiet current of her thoughts.

"We found someone!"

The shout tore through her brain. They quickly sent the camera down, chasing the survivor's voice. Everything was time then. Time was their most precious supply in the face of unknown injury, thirst, and an unknown number of victims still unfound. Elle took part in removing the block of cement preventing them from reaching the victim. It felt chalky when they drilled the tools into it, and they had to be careful not to break it apart and cause it to fall on him. His muffled voice grew clearer, and soon they saw him.

Something in Elle trembled when she saw the man, covered in dust and still in danger, his eyes shut from the sudden flood of light.

"Are you injured?" The captain asked, pronouncing each word with care.

"My leg is trapped," he responded.

The sun shone viciously at the group of rescuers removing debris from the unfortunate man's leg. The air grew dense with focus as they fought, determined to save a life. They managed to dispose of the stones. Elle felt streams of sweat trickle down her back from the heavy work, her undershirt clinging to the moist skin. As a child, she used to think that in moments of intense determination she'd stop feeling the minuscule details of her body—no scratching, itching, or other discomfort. With time, she discovered that even during the most intense action she still felt everything – only it didn't matter. It blended into the overall wave of sensations that had to be actively disregarded.

They had him. Finally, they managed to get a hold of the victim and carry him toward the medical team. Elle was one of the two who gave him over to Maya's team, and he was quickly hydrated and taken care of and soon dispatched to the hospital. Maya gave Elle a subtle nod, which Elle interpreted as *good job*, and which made her lips twitch in an imperceptible smile. It was good to have Maya around, the constant affirmation that nothing bad had happened to her.

There were many more people buried on the site, and the firefighters took turns going in, listening to the engineers' and architects" advice, taking the dogs, letting cameras into all the inaccessible parts of the crumbled structure. Some people were found dead and were left to be collected after all those who could be saved were pulled out.

It was becoming apparent that the operation involving the apartment complex would take much more time than first predicted due to some mistake regarding the number of victims inside. Elle was asked to stay overtime, and her team worked tirelessly to pull every living person out. When they got to the fourth floor structure, more sensitive ears picked up on a string of voices coming from somewhere near Elle's feet. They quickly let the cameras follow, and a family of three was discovered.

Again, the rescuers quickened their pace and employed every available device to help get the family out. Soon, their voices stopped being muffled and could now be heard clearly due to an unblocked passage in between.

"Hurry, please. Our daughter has a high fever!"

"We'll prioritize getting to your daughter, then. You two will be right after her," Captain Hunter shouted through the opening.

They dug and maneuvered, finally carrying the little girl out. She dropped in and out of consciousness and was quickly carried away to the hospital. When the team managed to get the couple out, the moon was already shining bright above their heads, accompanying the parents to the hospital, being driven to join their daughter and heal.

Elle had never been this exhausted before, her

knees giving out and her feet pulsing with pain. Captain Hallie Hunter came up to her, patting her on the shoulder. "Rodriguez." She looked at Elle with no effort to hide her own exhaustion in an effort to show comradery. "Take a break. Go home and show up on the scene tomorrow, hmm?" She nodded, leaving Elle alone.

Maya's team was also preparing to be changed. They were packing their equipment and preparing to return to the hospital, replaced by some other ambulance. Maya waved Elle over, standing to the side of the car. Elle came up, her steps heavy and dragging along the dirt. Face to face, neither of them knew what to say after what they'd just seen and lived through. Maya's lips twitched in that painfully familiar manner prognosing tears. Elle could do nothing but spread her arms in invitation, a silent nod to their shared path as rebuilders of the city and a silent hope that the common goal would forge a new bond between them, one stronger than before. She kept her arms open for as long as it took Maya to accept, because she knew Maya would accept. It was written on her face, in her body language, and in her eyes. For a moment they stood apart, then Maya let herself fall into Elle's arms. Elle once again felt as if she were holding something precious, a brilliant piece of the world, and what's more, she could bring her comfort. Her undershirt was soaked in something different than sweat – Maya began silently shaking, delicate shivers not so different than the rustling of leaves, and her warm tears soaked Elle's clothes.

"We'll be fine," Elle whispered. "We really will."

Although she knew Maya wasn't crying only because of that. There is only so much destruction one can witness and not feel a piece of them shatter. There is only so much rescue work one can do before one feels defeated. Only feeling defeated wouldn't help anyone – and there were still people to be saved. Elle gently pulled Maya away from herself, holding her shoulders tightly.

"We will help them, as much as we can. Get rest now. Go home, all right?"

Then they embraced one more time, and Maya was gone, getting into the ambulance with her team and driving away. Elle's eyes teared up again. This time she was unsure whether it was relief, exhaustion, overwhelm, or something else entirely. Her clothes smelled horribly, and she knew she'd better rest before the next day of work, which would be just as demanding. She gathered a few other firefighters dismissed for the day and climbed up to her usual driver's seat – but the road ahead seemed infinitely tiring, and her eyelids grew dangerously heavy.

"Can someone change me this time?" She raised the question, looking around the car.

"I can do it." O'Malley nodded, getting out to switch seats.

On the way home, Elle fought bravely not to let her eyes close. But passing through the disheveled city, there wasn't much she wanted to look at. She'd witnessed enough during this one day already, and she knew many more would come. Many buildings could still collapse. The city was growing empty, too. Many families had taken their children and had gone away to wait for safer times, to avoid looking the ugliness of disaster in the face.

12

MAYA

"Are you sure you're in a safe building, all of you?" Maya tried getting through to her parents for a thousandth time, but as usual, they wouldn't listen.

"Maya, the earthquake is over. What are you talking about?"

"Yes, but it could've created cracks in the structure of your building, and it might cause collapse later down the line, even tomorrow, for all you know, if you don't get that checked."

"I think we'd know if our building had cracks in it." Maya's father sounded as insufferable as always. "We're fine."

"Please get it checked." Maya sighed.

Ever since her parents had gotten back

together, talking to them had proved even more futile than when they'd been separated. After brisk goodbyes, they hung up. The familiar sense of hollowness stirred within her stomach, but she had no time for that. She had to call her brother, then go to work, go and witness again and again how cruel nature could be in its impartiality.

"Colin." Maya said his name, almost starving for an affectionate conversation.

"Hey *Mike*, how are you feeling? Are you horribly overworked?" Colin's voice contained a warm shade of worry, very different than their parents'' cold, harsh one that almost spelled *you should be ashamed I even have to worry about you.*

"I am, but every rescue worker is right now. I'll be heading back out in some twenty minutes. I wanted to discuss something with you, though."

"Be careful out there. Don't let them work you to an early grave. What is it?"

"I need you to check whether the building our parents are living in now is still safe to stay at, because they won't listen to me about possible cracks the earthquake could have caused. And I can't be rescuing my own parents from the building's ruins, all right? I'm having enough of that," Maya had let the irritation spill into her voice, and once she realized it, she felt a little ashamed. She wasn't annoyed with her job, only with her parents' stubbornness.

"Are you really okay?"

"I'm just sick of our parents never listening to me as if I don't know what I'm doing. I know natural disasters quite well," Maya sighed.

"I'll talk to them. Be safe, and good luck with the rescue. You're doing important work there."

Hanging up, Maya stood motionless for a moment, simply listening to herself breathe. Elle would probably be on the same scene with her, and once again they'd work side by side. Maya liked the perspective of that. She felt safe with Elle around, even if sometimes watching her work along the dangerously crumbling still pieces of the building caused sharp pangs of anxiety in her chest. They knew they could rely on each other's professionalism, though, and that wouldn't change. Elle's nerves of steel were infectious.

On the scene, ambulances stood lined up already, waiting to receive potential victims from floor number two. The lower the floor, the more dead people would be found, the ratio of dead to alive slowly increasing. And the dead, she knew, would have to wait until they helped rescue other buildings. She couldn't imagine what it would be like to know someone from her family had died. But she knew thinking about the dead in this situation was of no use when there were people out there still struggling to survive.

Elle's jacket shone brightly, RODRIGUEZ reflecting streaks of the sun among the backs of the other rescuers. The medics waited to be called either in case of a found victim or an injured rescuer.

Suddenly, Maya heard the dogs bark. Cameras and digging tools were employed to discover what had been the reason for the dogs' excitement. The firefighters gathered round the opening, but the digging took long hours. Then the rescuers quieted down. Maya couldn't see the reason from her post, and guesses flooded her thoughts. *They discovered corpses, but were expecting the living,* she thought on repeat. But no. Elle was carrying a child toward Maya's team.

"He's still breathing, he's still breathing," she shouted, carefully lying the boy down on one of their stretchers.

Preparing to take him to the hospital, they assessed his state—fractured ribs, potential pneumonia, severe dehydration – and that was probably not all. Maya remained on site and understood why the team had quieted down before. The boy would wake up as an orphan.

As they soon learned, he would also be the last person to be rescued from the building.

They began organizing themselves and regrouping, waiting for instructions. Maya found herself trying to get closer to Elle, seeking the comfort she'd experienced the last time against her chest, when they didn't need to talk, only breathe against each other and feel that the other person was alive.

"Hey." Maya approached the firefighting team, waving at Elle.

"Hey." Elle came up to her, dirt and sweat mixed on her face. "Feeling all right?"

"As much as one can." Maya nodded. "You? You were the one to find that small boy, right?"

"Yeah... And his parents... Well, our job is to

rescue those we can." She shook her head as if trying to straighten out her thoughts.

"It's fine to mourn. We're only human."

"Just not on the job." Elle nodded.

"No, not on the job, I guess." She stood silent for a while. "I hope we'll also do the next location together."

"Oh, yeah? Why?" Elle smiled lightly.

"I like working next to you." Maya mirrored her smile. "You're a good firefighter. I feel...secure."

"As if you're the one rescued." Elle laughed.

"RODRIGUEZ!" Captain Ramirez shouted to finally get Elle's attention. "We're moving to another collapse. Some survivors are said to be on scene. Let's get going!" And she disappeared into the truck.

"See you around." Elle squeezed Maya's shoulder affectionately and went to join her crew.

Indeed, Maya's team was assigned to the same scene as Elle. They drove only for a moment, since the buildings lay in the same neighbourhood, the worst prepared for a disaster of this type. Its buildings went down as if made out of paper, crumbling and trapping the sleeping citizens. The majority of work there had already been done, and the firefighters began their consultations with specialists regarding the possible survivors.

"It's been over a hundred hours already," someone said. "The chances are slim."

Either way, the rescue had to be performed as a rescue operation until they could be certain there was no one alive within the ruins. Maya and her colleagues felt uncomfortable only waiting, but each understood that at the end of the day, that was their mission as the firefighters' support. They spied on the unravelling of the very slow search operation, knowing that this time, it was better to be needed. They all hoped they'd be needed, observing the tall machines move away the rubble, undress the fallen building, and spread open its ribs. Now and then, Maya would see RODRIGUEZ flash somewhere on the familiar jacket.

"Building on Terrence Avenue fell due to post-earthquake vibrations, we need all available teams there," sounded in everyone's radios.

Maya knew there would be much to do now. Certainly many people would need surgery on the spot. Their ambulance rushed through the streets full of alarm and vigor.

On the scene, the police were trying to make the gathered crowd disperse. Many eyes were stuck to the site of tragedy, making the job of scanning the building difficult.

This was torture for Maya. She knew there were people in the building crawling, suffering, waiting for help, but there was no way of getting them out before making sure the operation was safe. So everyone waited until the scanning was over, until they could be told where to go. The building was only three stories, which meant high chances of survival.

Finally, the search went in to rescue the survivors. Elle and other firefighters dug through the rubble assisted by many automated tools that made the search easier. They located someone alive on the third level of the building, someone conscious and screaming.

Once the victim had been pulled out, Maya knew what to do. Major trauma to the head. Finally, she had the chance to help someone directly. The surgery went smoothly. The woman was young and would probably recover rather quickly once they sent her off to the hospital. Maya felt tired but invigorated. What a good feeling to find someone alive, someone lucky enough to be pulled out just in time. The search went on further, bringing many more victims to her and her colleagues. Due to the swiftness of their response, it seemed that most inhabitants of the building, if not all, had made it out alive. The work was difficult, but for Maya, it went by in such a state of focus that she hadn't even noticed when her superior let her know that her time operating was up and she should rest for the remainder of the day.

On her way home, she felt more optimistic than in the previous days. She felt powerful to be able t o save people, and that was the exact feeling which had pushed her toward this career.

13

ELLE

The sun was quickly going down, diminishing visibility on the scene. Elle felt her jaw tremble with strain from unconsciously tightening it. Every step was a gamble at this height, and they'd gone in too quickly to prepare harnesses. It was a risky choice, she knew, but the captain felt helpless in the face of the number of victims trapped by the upper layers of the building.

They were looking for survivors without dogs this time. It would be too difficult to get them up there. So the group moved carefully, probing every possible space with a camera. They were tired, and Elle could see that. One firefighter, however, somehow retained all her energy. She was an addition to this operation from another department, and a kid, really—twenty-one or twenty-two years old, Elle couldn't remember. Her overeagerness could get them into trouble, however. Uncareful steps could collapse the building on one of the survivors.

"Eh, Maria!" Elle tried calling her over. "Maria, come over here."

The young rescuer swiftly approached, repeating exactly the thing Elle had been worried about.

"You can't walk this way here. Who taught you this?" Elle quickly realized Maria might take the question literally. "No don't answer that. Walk the same way I do, all right? We don't want to collapse it further."

"I didn't know I was doing it wrong," Maria earnestly answered, looking at Elle. "Thanks."

Elle nodded, going back to her position in the search. Now and then she'd hear an indelicate step and knew exactly whose it was. *What is she doing here?* She grew angry. This was certainly no place for rookies, even if the city was desperate for help. There was no way this girl had any previous experience in this type of field, and she could certainly compromise the mission.

Elle got on the radio. "Captain Hunter?"

"Rodriguez."

"Firefighter Maria Smith is unfit for this operation. She's inexperienced in this type of a rescue operation."

There was silence on the line. Perhaps Hunter was asking around who this firefighter Smith was. But just as Elle heard her radio fire up again, the worst of her fears came true in a terrifying instant.

Many sounds came to her seemingly at once. A slipping stone. A scream. A crash. Shouting from below. Hunter commanding them from the radio to come down at once and pause the mission. Elle's head spun, trying to follow it all with a string of thought, to somehow tie together the hideous reality in a bow of understanding.

She was down on solid earth again but didn't remember having come down. Everything happened around her so fast. There were thin streaks of dried blood on the pavement next to the building. The moon was showing its head from above the buildings, and the cold sheets of moonlight rendered everything in Elle's surroundings even more absurd.

"Rodriguez." Captain Hunter wanted to continue, but the sentence seemed to lump in her throat. She came up to Elle and embraced her. "Our department will have to take over completely now, Smith's--" she stumbled, "Smith's department will have to take care of...the death."

Death echoed around Elle's mind. "What death?"

Hunter looked at Elle in concerned. "You're in shock."

"Did Maria die?" Elle knew someone had fallen, but she didn't know where that had led, or at least her mind was shutting it away.

"Yes. She slipped and unfortunately died on the spot."

A wave of something that could only be described as unreality overcame Elle. The *you should go home for now, Elle,* sounded as if from behind a thick wall—distant, irrelevant. What a terrible thought that a firefighter was actually dead on this mission. Her feet felt glued to the ground. That had never happened to her before. No firefighter she knew had ever died, and definitely not right in front of her. Everyone around her moved hurriedly from place to place, arranging another rescue operation or talking about letting the proper offices know about *the death*. Elle didn't know what to do with herself. She wanted to be close to the other ones who'd been on the roof, but she realized they were from the other department —the one which was now in mourning.

After some time passed, she couldn't tell how much, she realized Hunter had dismissed her for the day. She felt strange being treated this way, as if she had the right to mourn a firefighter from another department who she had known for half an hour before *the death*. She was in shock. She knew it. She ordered an uber, which took time to go around the blockades. She had to run up to him from a long distance due to the police barricading the scene.

She still had her firefighter's jacket on, everything besides the helmet and tools, in fact. She looked ridiculous inside the small car.

"Is everything all right, ma'am?" The driver smiled shyly in the rearview mirror.

She nodded, not knowing what to say Elle was nauseated and was focusing all her strength on not vomiting inside the car. The task surprisingly helped her calm down, the singular thought only of *do not vomit* kept her mind in a unified stream.

She got out of the car in front of her house, weak-legged and feeling as if everything around her was unreal. Standing there for some time, she realized she had no keys with her. Her bag was still at the station. This completely overwhelmed her. The station seemed so far gone she diddn't even know where to begin.

Her phone rang, dragging her out of the daze.

"Elle?" Maya's voice was gentle.

"Mhmm." Elle nodded.

"Are you okay? Where are you?" Slight worry rose in Maya's tone, but it remained steady and calm, and Elle wished she would just keep talking, keep the flow of her words like the steady rise and fall of the sea.

"I'm standing in front of my house."

"Why not inside of it, Darling?"

"I don't have my keys." Elle's own voice sounded to her as if from a deep well in the ground, abstract and wobbly.

"..Can I drive up to get you? I'm just finished for today, and I feel as if something bad has happened to you."

"Something bad has happened." Elle nodded. *Something very bad has happened.*

"I'm on my way. Wait for me. All right? I'm coming."

Elle heard the sound of the call ending, and she simply nodded at the night air all around her. Tired, she sat down on the lawn in front of her house. The dewy grass wet her pants, but they were so thick that she didn't notice. She probably wouldn't have no matter what. The moon appeared gigantic, as unreal as the whole evening. A car parked right in front of her, and its light had a blinding harshness to it.

Elle sat at the corner of Maya's couch wearing Maya's t-shirt and her underwear. Maya had thrown all Elle's clothes besides the thick, outer uniform into her washing machine, which was now spinning them in endless circles, bubbly and moist.

Elle was holding a cup of chamomile tea with milk, and through the thick fog she hadn't managed to get rid of, bubbles of nostalgia kept showing their little heads and then disappearing again in the depths of anxiety.

"Can I help you?" Maya sat at the other end of the couch, worried but compassionate.

Elle shook her head. "I heard her scream when she fell. Her name was Maria, and it's so much worse that I knew her name."

Maya nodded. "That sounds horrible."

"It is horrible. She was twenty-two, or maybe even twenty-one." Elle looked at Maya. "No one should die this young."

"No, they shouldn't." Maya spread her arms. "Would you like to come closer?"

Elle nodded. She crawled toward Maya, resting her face against Maya's chest, making herself comfortable in her embrace. Their breathing soon unified, a constant flowing up and down, up and down. Elle knew she wouldn't sleep. Her body felt jittery and on edge.

"You can go to sleep," she said to Maya. "Thank you for this."

"Are you feeling better?"

A thousand thoughts flashed through Elle's head, and she felt she was, indeed, regaining clarity of mind. Her thoughts were nothing pleasant, however. Elle felt as if there had been a clear way for her to prevent the accident. She also felt out of place in her grief, since she hadn't known the firefighter. She decided to keep those thoughts to herself, not burdening Maya with them. She needed to get back on track and back to work.

"I need to get back to work."

Maya's embrace tightened around her.

"Elle, you don't have to go to work right away."

"But I do. That's exactly what happens. She wasn't even from my department, and they will all be working tomorrow." Elle twisted her head to look up at Maya. "That's what it means to have this job during a crisis."

Maya brushed Elle's hair from her face in a gentle gesture, and Elle felt herself melt into this newly established kindness. They remained silent for a while, simply appreciating their breaths mingling together.

"Can I tell you something serious?" Maya asked quietly after a while.

"What is it?"

"It wasn't your fault the girl fell."

Elle stirred on the couch, quickly rising from it. Her heartbeat quickened, and she was trying not to shout.

"Don't tell me that," she looked at Maya intensely. "I appreciate you driving me here and everything, but don't pretend to know what happened."

Maya sat quietly, her chest rising and falling in rhythm with her quick breaths. "I don't want to argue with you," she said after a moment.

"Then don't lie," Elle snapped, sitting down in the middle of the couch. "Don't lie, because it was my fault. I saw that she wasn't prepared, and I should've gotten her down before. Or I should've watched her more closely. But I told Hunter too late, and now she's gone."

She sighed deeply, adding, "But it doesn't matter now, does it? She's gone. I need to bear this guilt until the end, but it's my own thing to deal with. I hope her family is all right."

Maya sat still.

"That's stupid. I know they aren't," Elle added, feeling her speech grow more erratic and nonsensical. She no longer knew what she had wanted to say. She only knew she didn't want to scare Maya away. She really needed her close. "Maya," she said in a whisper, because her throat had grown tight. "Could you come close again?"

And she did, embracing Elle again, uniting their breathing.

"Would you like to move to my bedroom?" Maya asked after a while.

Elle nodded. "But I can also sleep on the couch, if you'd prefer that."

"Why would I prefer that?" Maya smiled.

"Well, I don't know. I still don't know what you think about me now."

Maya looked at Elle, understanding. "I think that's a conversation for another night."

And Elle understood.

They fell asleep quickly, both exhausted and infected by the feverish atmosphere of grief. Grief for Maria, and grief for all the victims as well, nameless to their minds yet still carrying the weight of death with them, the silent thickness of tragedy in the air. Their sleep was of the deepest kind, the kind children experience. The type that bodies craving restoration spin at night, covering the minds of the restless with a thick web of dreams, elaborate images that stretch and pull on the mind, the kind one forgets in the morning as soon as a window gets in the way.

Elle showed up to the station struggling to harness the disarray of her state. She arrived late in yesterday's half-dried clothes, with yesterday's conversations on her mind. She soon realized that everything appeared out of joint—the firefighters as well as the captains appeared equally distracted, overcoming some internal chaos.

There was word going around about the deceased firefighter—various hypotheses and rumors, spread about by those absent from the scene who had heard through the news and word of mouth. Those who had been on the scene tried quieting the rumors down, tried swallowing their own grief like a pill without any water to help it go down. Elle understood that their work was to become even more difficult than it had been before.

She noticed a bunch of her friends talking in hushed voices around the corner.

"I heard she was the daughter of so-and-so, and that's how she got to be on such a high-risk mission so early..."

Elle came up to them from the back, saying, "Johnson, you always make so much sense, don't you? I'm sure it makes sense for a father to make his daughter take part in situations where she's more likely to die. That's so clever of you to say!" She was getting ahead of herself but was oddly enjoying the ride and the release it provided.

"That's just what I've heard, anyway." Johnson shrugged.

"Don't parrot random shit that you hear, then." Elle wasn't done. "It's offensive to speak of the dead this way, so if you have nothing respectful to say, I'd rather you'd just stay quiet."

"Jesus." Haley sighed, essentially putting the last nail to her coffin.

"The fuck do you roll my eyes at me for?" Elle's face grew redder.

"I didn't-"

"Did you know that she was younger than you?"

Haley clearly didn't. Her face froze, and she slowly shook her head.

"Yeah. Significantly younger, like twenty-one. Died on the spot. So shut up about her. Just shut up. I don't want to hear you--"

"Rodriguez!" Ramirez's voice cut through the argument.

"Yes, captain?" Elle turned around to face her.

"Come with me to my office, now."

Elle nodded and left Haley and the crowd

without another word. She obediently followed Ramirez to the office, closing the door behind her as instructed. She didn't know what to expect and didn't much care. Her mind was so on edge that she barely could understand the consequences of anything. They sat down facing each other.

"Why are you starting fights with your fellow firefighters?" Ramirez began with no bullshit, as was her habit.

"I wasn't starting a fight, captain," Elle asserted. "I was trying to stop the festering rumors from spreading."

"People will always talk, Rodriguez. Let them talk. We have more important--"

"More important things than respecting to dead in the line of duty for our fellow firefighter?" Her eyes welled with tears, but she bravely tried to contain her voice in one piece.

Ramirez understood something then, something that had apparently been lacking before. She slowly nodded.

"You were there, weren't you?"

"Did you not know?" Elle felt anger and irritation spread all around her limbs.

"No. I'd left by the time the tragic accident happened. But you were still there?"

"I--" Elle felt her throat tighten again, but she pushed through, "It was my fault that she fell."

"What do you mean?" Ramirez leaned in toward Elle. "What do you mean exactly?"

"I saw that she wasn't well prepared for this situation, and I called Hunter too late. I could've kept a better eye on her."

Ramirez quickly stopped her, raising her hand. "Elena, you need to cut this out. What happened, happened. It's a hideous reality, but it happened. You know that's not truly your fault. You went above and beyond in informing the captain of your suspicions. That's all you could've done."

She got up from her chair, and Elle swiftly followed.

"But now we need to get back to work, kid," she said in a gentler tone. "We all need to get back to work."

Out of the office, Elle passed by Haley without a word. Soon, a meeting would be called to establish a new plan of action regarding the structures still affected by the earthquake. Sitting through a meeting was the last thing Elle felt she'd want to do. She was restless, her bones itching for movement, for action. Her hazy four-hours-of-sleep mind called for fresh air. They were all going insane with the effort, and adding to that grief, Elle could see their strength waning. But there was no one else to put the city back together. No one else could do their job, even though departments from all neighboring cities were being driven to Phoenix Ridge day by day. They'd need to establish a system of cooperation.

During the meeting, her thoughts briefly jumped to the night spent with Maya. She barely remembered it, as if through fog. The sounds of the washing machine tumbling her clothes about, the scent of chamomile tea with a generous portion of milk, Maya's steady heartbeat against her face. She felt lucky that Maya still cared about her that much. Or perhaps not *still*. Maybe they'd begun caring for each other anew?

"Rodriguez, focus." Captain Hunter called her back to the meeting. Her gaze was kind, however. Their shared part in the tragedy had quietly brought them closer to each other, a thread of understanding tying them together.

Elle nodded and remained attentive throughout the remainder of the meeting. There was a team to be dispatched to secure a cluster of buildings on the verge of crumbling and help safely evacuate the inhabitants.

She knew the task was simple, yet Elle couldn't stop her fear. She knew she had to choke down the feeling, eat it up and never bring it back, but when her hands trembled, it felt difficult. Even while driving, she felt wrong. Her body was refusing to perform its usual tasks, making it difficult to focus on the road, but she had to do it. They were very close. Everything felt like an effort for Elle, but she knew herself to be strong. She trusted herself to handle it.

The three buildings had been built according to the old safety standards and were now incredibly unstable due to cracking caused by the earthquake and the vibrations that followed. They still cropped up here and there throughout the city. Not even twenty hours had passed since the accident. Elle kept thinking, kept counting the time. What for? She couldn't say.

Huge arms of machines were put in place to help hold the buildings, their imposing size eclipsing all the fire trucks around. These machines would be of some help, though they couldn't hold the buildings together from the inside, which was now the main concern.

The rescue teams received information that the staircase in one building was damaged, trapping some residents inside. The firefighters were preparing to go in, including Elle, when a large chunk of the wall fell down right next to them.

"Fuck." Elle stood frozen, looking at the wall fragment lying dangerously close to her. There was a huge commotion, captains ordering the firefighters back.

"This is too dangerous." Captain Hunter shook her head. "You're not going in."

The team was stopped, and everyone went back to a safe distance from the collapsing building. It was a race against time once more.

"We're going to evacuate them out the windows." Captain Ramirez nodded. "We need to prepare the truck ladders. All the drivers, get inside the trucks."

Elle listened, going into the truck. She would have to spend a long time maneuvering to get to the perfect position. The people would have to walk down the ladder. She was hoping everyone could.

Ramirez was giving her instructions, which window to target, what distance. Elle strained her eyes, looking back and to the sides with an intensity she had not had to employ before. Her understanding of the car from all the years driving had to come through. But she managed. Hhe stopped the truck. The ladder began reaching out to the third floor window.

A young woman with a child tethered to her back began walking down. The child was crying loudly, and the sound echoed from the building nearby, creating an even more nervous atmosphere. But the woman finally safely reached the pavement. She was quickly taken care of by the medics, not because she was injured but because of the shock all inhabitants had suffered. Elle kept the ladder stretched out until all the third floor residents were safely down on the ground. They huddled in blankets given out by medics and watched as their house cracked, held together by mechanic claws. What would happen once the machines were removed?

The second floor went just as successfully, and the first floor was reached by a normal ladder leaning against the building. Everyone was successfully evacuated, and the question of what would happen to the building would find its resolution.

"It will have to be destroyed," one of the engineers began explaining to the terror-stricken crowd. "We have to do it before it falls apart and causes more damage."

Elle's crew was moving to help the next one out of the three, but she couldn't help listening in. These people had thought they were lucky having escaped the earthquake's first wave, and now they were learning that their home must be destroyed.

What a time. She shook her head, joining the rest of the crew.

The next buildings were rescued similarly. Elle twisted and turned her head to maneuver the truck around, the people went down on ladders, and the day was neared evening. As the sun began to set, and Elle sat behind the wheel waiting for the victims to descend the ladder, she thought about Maria's family. Maria would get the full honors funeral, with trucks, apparatus, orchestra, and everything. Some family members from abroad would come, kids who probably had never even known her and would not feel the grief that her parents would have to endure throughout the entire ceremony.

"RODRIGUEZ!" Hunter was suddenly at her window, startling Elle.

"What, Captain?"

"We've been trying to reach you for the past five minutes. This is unacceptable. Get a hold of yourself and get out of the truck!"

"Yes, Captain." Elle got out of the truck.

Her face was on fire. She had never failed something as simple as hearing instructions, and the taste of shame on her tongue was as new to her as it was infuriating. O'Malley replaced her as the driver. The whole way back, Elle felt her heartbeat in her throat. She couldn't understand what was happening to her, why this weakness wouldn't go away.

"You need to get a grip on this, Rodriguez." Hunter touched Elle's back in a gesture Elle guessed was supposed to show understanding, even if it mainly came off as pity. "It's difficult for everyone who was there, but we still have work to do."

"I don't know what you're talking about, Captain," Elle said coldly. She was fed up with this situation and Hunter's pitiful looks.

"I think you do."

The rest of the way back to the firehouse was spent in silence.

Back home, Elle could finally change, and the scent of fresh clothes made her feel cleaner, more whole. She wanted to check the news coverage of Maria's death but changed her mind. She didn't need to see what others were saying. She'd been there. She knew everything she had to, and now she simply had to forget it all.

She found a bottle of whiskey in the fridge. *p Perfect,* she thought while settling on her couch. Her limbs felt heavy and sore, as if gravity had doubled and was keeping her glued to the spot. The ice in her glass popped, a familiar, lonely sound, and she finally, truly felt at home.

Until her ringtone cut through the silence. She let the sharp, steady ringing sound around the house for a while. She sank deeper into the couch, knowing that sooner or later she had to pick up, but *not just yet.*

The ringing ceased.

"Fuck this." Elle grunted, getting up to get to the phone. It was Maya. Elle decided to call back.

"Hi," she said when Maya picked up in the span of a second.

"Hey," she heard Maya's eager, though tired, voice. "I wanted to ask how you're feeling after yesterday."

"Are you at work?"

"I'm on a break, but yes, I'll be working until late."

Elle exhaled, thinking how much she wanted to be completely honest with Maya, and on the other hand, how weak that would make her feel. She didn't know how to have this conversation.

"So, how are you?"

"Had a bit of tension with Hunter today," Elle admitted despite herself.

"Oh, I'm sorry to hear that. What happened?" Maya's voice was so patient that Elle's own thoughts became less confused and tangled. She felt ready to tell her everything.

"I guess I'm... I wasn't very attentive today. I don't know why I can't get a grip. I don't hear people well, and I keep drifting away."

"Elle, this is serious. You can't be working in this state, you know that?"

Elle shook her head violently. "No, don't say that. I'll be better tomorrow."

"Oh, honey." Maya sighed. Elle felt strange, hearing all these mannerisms and words directed at her again, as if they'd gone back in time, as if the past years hadn't happened. "It's not your fault for feeling this way. It's a completely normal reaction. You can't control it."

Elle sat down, not knowing what to say anymore. She felt as if she'd stepped into quicksand out of which no one could help her out. "I'd like to just forget about all this, go back to the way it was."

"You'll feel better with time, but you need to take it slowly now."

"I can't, Maya. I have to work. I don't get special treatment, I wasn't the only one there."

"Well, it doesn't matter. You're a danger to yourself and others now." Maya's voice grew suddenly stern. "You have to take a break."

"What did you just say?" Elle was shocked.

"You're a brilliant firefighter, Elle, and the strongest person I know. But you've been traumatized by what happened and can't focus. Isn't that deadly in your line of work?"

Elle took a few gulps of whiskey. She knew Maya was right, and she knew that arguing with her would prove utterly useless. But she also felt that admitting to that, admitting that she couldn't work, would put her in an impossible position, threatening everything she'd worked so hard for.

"I don't want to argue with you," she said quietly.

"I don't want you to keep being afraid of seeming weak. Having problems is not being weak, Elle, ignoring them is. I thought you'd work that out by the time you were thirty."

"Whatever. If I can't open up to you, just say it," Elle threw into the conversation carelessly, feeling that to expect a good outcome out of this conversation would be like tossing a six-sided die and praying for a seven.

"That's manipulative."

They fell silent. Elle was afraid of that word, afraid of seeming like her father, behaving like him. She knew she could sometimes, and she knew she did it now.

"I'm sorry. You're right."

Maya sighed. "I know this is a sensitive subject for you. I don't want you to feel like I'm overstepping or trying to seem like I know best. But this situation right now is serious, and I know that you see it, too. Please think about this and talk to your superiors if necessary. I need to go now."

After saying goodbye to her, Elle felt completely depleted. There was not much she felt she could do besides finishing her drink and going to sleep. At a time like this, no one would take Maya's concerns seriously. They were still in the middle of dragging the city out from the disastrous effects of the earthquake and needed every firefighter on deck. Besides, she hadn't even known Maria closely. She hadn't even been from her department. She had no claim to this grief.

The journal lay on the edge of the coffee table, staring at Elle. She felt there were no words she could put in there to help herself now, nothing that could soothe her besides pretending nothing had happened. Tipsy, she went to take a long shower, feeling the water hit her back in pleasant streams. Feeling pure again. At home, she felt as if nothing had to be real. Everything concerning the outside world floated away into obscurity.

She began thinking about her relationship with Maya in recent days. How worried and caring Maya had been, and quite effortlessly so. She wished it could be this way not only in times of crisis, that they would carry it out of this difficult time and into normal life. Most of all, she wished she could care for Maya too right now, instead of what had been happening for the past two days. But then again, she knew she would always feel bad receiving help.

Seeing her bed, she remembered the previous night at Maya's place. The repeated sounds of screaming and crashing against the pavement had woken her up throughout the night, causing her to sweat and disorienting her. She tried thinking it would be different in her own bed, that they would pass. Closing her eyes, she already knew that wouldn't be true, but the exhaustion in her body dragged her to sleep nonetheless.

14

MAYA

Two days after her phone conversation with Elle, Maya was called to another disaster site. One of the shopping mall buildings had partially collapsed following the unnoticed cracking in the structure of its first floor. It was the city's biggest tragedy following the earthquake itself, with a speculated hundreds of victims trapped within the crushed structure.

All firefighting and medical units available were called in for the rescue mission, with time being their most precious asset. The quick response of the city made the chances of victims' survival high, and Maya, speeding through the city in the ambulance, was as focused as ever.

The scene looked apocalyptic. The large building stood tilted and crashed, and the rescue units were so small in comparison that they looked like ants swarming around its base. Everyone knew the rescue would take weeks and would eat up most of the city's emergency resources. Maya's crew was placed, as they often were, in collaboration with Elle's fire department.

Soon, the ambulance began receiving the first victims, the people close to the exits whose rescue didn't evolve the risk of entering the crumbling structure. Maya received tens of trauma victims. She and her colleagues rushed in to operate and send them out to the nearest hospitals. Maya's clothes were soon stained with multiple people's blood mingling together on the fabric. Her face dripped with sweat out in the open sun, but the rescue was going efficiently. The engineers were scanning the building in hopes of entering soon, knowing that a wrong decision regarding that could cost the rescuers' lives. The atmosphere was heated.

The rotation of ambulances wasn't ideal. It meant the equipment needed for certain injuries was sometimes lacking and the crew had to wait a few minutes. The nearby hospitals had begun setting up a provisory base on the grounds near the scene. Still sometimes they'd have to drive someone off to an actual hospital if the situation was dire. The disinfectant was running low, and the medics were afraid they'd soon run into problems. Maya admitted another trauma victim, knowing they'd have to wait to drive him to the hospital, so it was her job to stabilize his state the best she could. Within the ambulance, she was lacking a nurse. They struggled without the third person, but Maya pushed through, desperate to save the man, who was in grave condition. He writhed from pain, but she knew she would soon be done, if only she had one more pair of hands. But no matter. She managed to sew him up and his state greatly improved, enough for him to wait for transport in the space of the ambulance.

. . .

Outside of the car, Maya noticed the team of rescuers preparing to go in. They were discussing the strategy. It was a team of six plus dogs. Maya's eyes greedily went from face to face, looking for what she'd been fearing the most. And there she was. Maya's heart sank down to her stomach. Elle was one of the rescuers that were going in.

Another surgeon called her over to assist him, and she had to force herself to tear her eyes away from the group. She went into the ambulance, feeling the heavy beating of her heart, feeling her fingers go numb. The person in the ambulance had a fractured rib cage, and they needed another opinion regarding some difficult decision. Maya gave it her best, analyzing the victim's state and discussing it with her colleagues before assisting them in the operation. But her mind felt foggy, felt detached.

She couldn't stop thinking about Elle's recent problems and the high-risk operation on which she was about to embark. Or maybe had already done so. Maya wouldn't know. She ran out of the ambulance once she was no longer needed, searching for any clue as to how the rescue was going. It appeared to be going fine, according to plan. The Captain was on the radio with the crew in a deep state of focus.

Then it happened.

Something went wrong. Suddenly, the people monitoring the rescuers inside looked at each other, stressed. Maya could feel in her chest that something was terribly wrong with Elle. Captain Hunter was shouting *evacuate from the building*, and Maya felt as if she were underwater, every sound and sensation could barely reach her, ringing in her ears.

Hunter said to someone standing next to her, "They've got issues coming out."

The worst nightmares were coming true for Maya. She could do nothing but wait for the crew to get out, to check Elle's state for herself, to see whether

her cruel premonition had been right and whether Elle was injured. Hunter was instructing the firefighters in a tone of calm urgency. Additional cameras went inside in hopes of locating the team. Two of the search dogs ran out of the ruin.

"Did you follow the dogs? They're out!" Hunter raised her voice through the radio. After a while, she repeated the response. "No, they lost them."

Everyone was on the edge of their seats, biting their nails and sweating from stress. Six people they'd sent in couldn't get out of the still unstable building. Everyone's attention was directed toward bringing them out, afraid that they might have destabilized the construction, and it would bury the rescuers alive, as well.

"We've got them on camera," one of the technicians shouted. "We know where they are."

. . .

Everyone breathed out the air they'd been holding in, hoping that from then on it'd be easy.

"There are two injured," he continued.

"Let's get them out as soon as possible." Hunter began discussing the safest way out with the team of firefighters and technicians, communicating everything to the team inside through radio.

This whole time, Maya stood motionless, absorbing every new piece of information like a bullet burning through her chest.

Someone showed through the opening. The firefighters ran to get them and help them out. As soon as the first woman was entirely out, the next followed, and then Maya saw her. Carried by two other firefighters, Elle was unconscious and bloodied. The sight of her limp body twisted Maya's heart, jolting her into action. She ran to get stretchers, and holding on to them with an ER medic, she ran to get Elle. She was in critical condition with suspected traumatic brain injury as well as severe bleeding from her thigh. Maya's mind worked on double the speed. They needed a blood transfusion for Elle STAT, as well as to get her on an operating table to assess and stabilize the injury to her head.

"We need blood, AB negative, quickly," Maya shouted at the other medic.

"Are you sure it's her--"

"YES, now get it STAT!"

Maya fastened Elle to the ambulance's operating table, ready to perform this surgery on her own, if no one else showed up quickly enough. Fortunately, that wasn't the case, and she got everything started properly. Then a dizzy spell took over her. This was Elle she was about to dive into the head of, cut open and sew up, see her damaged skull. But if she were to look for a replacement, they'd lose time that Elle really didn't have much of. No.

She had to push through. She'd pretend it was someone else. She had to get this right. The damage took her aback. This would be one of the most difficult things she'd ever done, and they were still waiting to get the blood. She couldn't begin operating without it.

Furious, she left the ambulance, looking for the medic.

"Where is the blood? We have to start operating, and we have nothing for her," she shouted, completely on the edge.

"I'm working on it, but we don't have the type here."

"Well then where's O negative?"

"We're running low, so I thought I'd--"

. . .

"Don't talk. Get me the blood. We don't have any in the ambulance anymore."

She went back inside to check Elle's state. The situation was dire, and she had to have the new supply of blood. At long last, the medic came back with bags of it.

"Finally!" Maya quickly began working.

She had to supply the ambulance's system with the new blood and get it flowing to Elle so they could start operating without any risks of making her bleed out. The time came where Elle's life depended completely on Maya's skill as a surgeon. She worked tirelessly without any sense of passing time, knowing that as long as she was applying everything she knew, Elle had a chance of surviving.

Stepping away from the table and letting the EMTs take her away and drive her away to the hospital,

Maya felt as if in a daze. Shakily, she stepped outside, unsure whether she was going to vomit or collapse.

"Dr. Monroe, are you not getting in?" Fleur pointed to the ambulance, encouraging.

"I still have work here--"

"Dr. Monroe, get in the ambulance. You should stay with her."

Maya understood and got back into the car. She stroked Elle's hand, terrifyingly limp, decorated with streaks of dried blood. While the ambulance sped through the traffic, sirens wailing, she thought how scary it must've been for Elle to see a building crumble above her head, to feel trapped within its collapsed walls. She couldn't bring herself to look at her face for too long. She knew she couldn't fall apart completely now. She had to stay strong, but the sight of Elle tethered to the operating table and unconscious was close to being too much for her mind.

The hospital was full to the brim, overcrowded. They said they couldn't admit another trauma patient. The crew was furious hearing that there'd been such a case of terrible miscommunication and bad organization. The hospital had been shown to them as available. They had to turn around and drive to the next closest one. Maya's nerves got the better of her, and she vomited into a plastic bag.

The next hospital admitted Elle. Maya ran in with the hospital's crew, unaware of time and space, aware only of the burning need to be close to Elle.

"What are you doing, Doctor?" The nurses looked at her, irritated and surprised.

"This is my partner," she managed to say.

. . .

"We will operate. You have to leave her now." The nurse took her by the hand, leading her out of the room.

Maya knew they'd have to actually fix Elle's head far beyond what she'd done back in the ambulance, but the thought of letting her go, of letting her be treated by other surgeons, terrified her. She sat in the waiting room, feeling her body go through a thousand stages of panic.

The hours went by, yet she sat still. She couldn't go back to work, not now. She wouldn't be able to. The only thing for her to do was to wait. Wait until they finished the surgery. Wait until Elle woke up.

"Dr. Monroe, where are you?" Her superior called her, sounding on edge himself.

. . .

"I'm sorry, my partner suffered a grave injury. I operated on her, and now she's in the hospital. I can't leave."

He had no choice but to let her be. This was no state in which to rescue people. She had to make sure that the person she cared about the most actually survived. In those hours, she knew Elle was the most important person in the world to her. She knew by the way her chest tightened as if to crush her heart when she saw her being carried out of the building. She'd never unlearn that.

The evening came, and the surgery was over. The first one, anyway. She knew they'd have to operate on Elle many times to get her back. The nurses stopped her from running into the room. *She needs rest. She needs rest.* They gave Maya a blanket and she drifted off to sleep.

15

ELLE

The jolts of pain came to her in waves at first. White foam of a teeth-grinding sensation would wash over her, then leave for a moment. In those moments in between, she would experience a rush of memories, some of them recent, some long forgotten, dug out from below the heaps of more relevant ones.

After a tiring wave of pain in her temples, she felt transported to an abandoned-by-her-consciousness beach. The white sand tickled her feet, the ocean's waves came and went in a constant whisper. The image brought her much solace, remembering the quiet morning hours, the rustling of the tent's walls when she would sneak away to run along the beach, lit by the early sun, licked by the tongues of waves.

For a long time, she didn't feel like a person, but rather a river of memories. The events of her life didn't seem to bear any connection to each other. Indeed, she couldn't think of trying to look for one. Instead, in a manner similar to that of dreams, they transported her from one place to another without any clear purpose, and the only thing she could do was to accept that as her reality, watch, as what had already unraveled did so again. Her mind existed as an eternity. There was no beginning of that state in her memory, and since she couldn't remember any other state of being, there was no reason for her to expect an end.

Some scenes she was thrust into troubled her, while others brought comfort. An exhausting slither of pain from her head down to her legs paralyzed Elle's thoughts for a moment, but soon it stopped mattering. Her hands were set firmly against a wooden surface. Her voice seemed to be raised, angry, but she couldn't understand why. Warm, dim light was falling down on her from a ceiling lamp. There was another person in the room. Her voice was equally as angry, like a storm hitting rocks on the shore.

"How could you have lied to me?"

"Fuck." Elle felt her hands go up to her temples, massaging them. She felt stressed. "It meant nothing, I told you already. I was drunk. It meant nothing."

"It meant *something* to me, Elle. Does that matter to you, still? And on top of everything, you lied straight to my face more than once!"

Elle's legs carried her around the room. She was only a spectator, observing from inside of her head. The words made their way out on their own. "What choice did I have? We can just move on from this, pretend it didn't happen."

The other person shook her head. Elle could see tears flowing down her face in little streaks.

"Maya," she said, coming up to her.

"I don't want to be with someone who is so casual about disrespecting me. If you can't stick to simple agreements, that truly shows your selfishness, Elle. And you know you can be selfish," Maya went to another room, out of sight.

Elle collapsed on the couch. Its softness contrasted with the sharp tangle of feelings tightening in her chest. She felt trapped within herself. She wanted to escape this place. She felt that the situation would not end well, would not be resolved within that room, and that weighed heavily on her.

But then she began slipping away, her consciousness melting into the familiar velvet black fabric of nonexistence, of pause in thought. The warmth of its embrace comforted her, carried her away from the pain of her body, high and far away, leaving her body behind, her heavy limbs too weighty for her consciousness to drag away with it. And then she sank into a state of non-being, without dreams or memories, without thought or perception. Only the body's mechanical rhythms remained, its steady rise and fall with each breath and exhale, and its ceaseless heartbeat, never abandoning its march onward.

She heard a mingling of sounds to the left. It took her some time to recognize the strings of sounds as voices, of various pitches and rhythms. For a while, it amused her to hold the threads of these voices in her mind. Not quite sure what she was supposed to do with them, she squeezed and stretched them out, felt the way they reached her. Some had a fuzzy quality to them, some more slick and oily, some raspy. She felt them nest in her mind, echo around or plunge deep.

Out of their nets emerged something she recognized only later, how the threads could be divided into chunks, little words. Uncovering the words brought her much amusement, every one word carried some image with it, like connecting tissue, like glue making collages out of the images.

Soon, she understood that the collages brought emotions with them, or new sets of memories. Like wagons, they created sentences, and the sentences played around with each other, bumped against each other like in a game of football. She made the space of her mind into a playing field, watched the threads of sounds knit words, words be glued into sentences, and the sentences be carried by trains of thought. Sometimes her understanding would be derailed. Sometimes there were too many sounds for her to follow. With time, however, out of the fog emerged full conversations.

"Will she ever fully recover?"

"The doctors aren't saying anything definitive yet."

"Is it true that her ex operated on her?"

Her ex carried something very emotional in it. Her thoughts stirred with a new substance in them, creating abstract patterns that soon descended into the reality of memories. She retrieved the figure of Maya from her memory.

The image of the living room anger floated back, as did many others. A warmth against her chest. A soothing voice. Recalling Maya brought a sudden richness to her thoughts, laden with feelings of various flavors. The recollections awakened her mind, and soon something overwhelming happened—she remembered the way to lift her eyelids, and a flood of light hurt her eyes.

"Oh my God, look! She's awake!" O'Malley pointed her finger at Elle, who, for the first time in days, regained consciousness and was now trying to process what had happened.

"Don't point fingers, that's rude." She smiled weakly.

The group of firefighters were on the verge of jumping for joy, hearing her voice. They started talking over each other, each having a question to ask, each wanting to tell Elle something important. She scanned the faces jumping around her and noticed a significant lack.

"Does Maya know I'm here?" she asked, her voice painfully weak.

Her friends looked around each other,

concerned and whispering. *Someone ,should probably call in the nurse. She doesn't sound well.* Johnson ran out to get someone. Captain Ramirez stepped closer to Elle, touching her hand with care.

"Maya was a part of the team who drove you here." She smiled. "She stayed in the waiting room for a long time before going back to her duties. We'll call her to come here as soon as she can for sure."

Elle blinked, surprised. "How do you two know each other?"

"We got to know each other here, actually, in the hospital visiting you." She nodded. "She's a really nice woman, Elle."

Elle's eyes teared up, so she twisted her head so as not to seem dramatic. Ramirez tactfully stepped back a little and looked away.

"Elle, you looked horrible when we got you out of the building, for real," Haley said, closing the door. "The nurse is on her way."

"You scared us all." Ramirez nodded. "You must be a really tough thing to have survived that."

Everyone agreed, looking at Elle with compassion. She felt awkward, almost pitied, and wanted to change the tone of the conversation as quickly as possible.

"To be honest, guys, I feel kind of shitty. I won't be able to help you anymore, and the city is still such a mess."

"Elle, I never took you for someone prone to self-pity," O'Malley said in a mocking tone of surprise but was quickly silenced by a critical look from Ramirez and the rest.

"You're right." Elle nodded, "That is self-pitiful. But I'm also trying to be honest."

"We've got a lot of firefighters. One, even as brilliant as you, won't make such a big difference," Ramirez said matter-of-factly, but her voice carried something gentle within it, something that truly reassured Elle.

She could only say *hmm,* to affirm Ramirez's words. But she was afraid that if she lets the words out of her mouth, she might feel like crying again. The situation overwhelmed her, and she felt weak in the face of it, unsure of how to react or cope. She didn't want to ask her friends to leave, but also the crowd around her hospital room wasn't helping.

When a doctor together with a nurse entered and asked everyone to leave, Elle felt awash in relief. With time, increased pain entered her consciousness, and her breathing became more erratic. She grew more tired by the minute.

"How are you feeling, Ms. Rodriguez?"

What followed was tiring and long, questions about feeling in various parts of her body, the level of pain, and her clarity of thought, and Elle began feeling endlessly sleepy, as if something was tugging on her sleeve and pulling her into an abyss of dreams, rest, calm. The doctor looked worried.

"Do you not feel that, Ms. Rodriguez?"

"What?" she asked, suddenly wide awake by the nervous feeling that something was wrong, based on the doctor's expression. Something had to be wrong, and she didn't know what.

"I'm touching your leg," he explained gently.

Elle looked down to where his hand was. He was indeed touching her leg, but she couldn't feel anything. She looked up at him, terrified, seeing her entire career dissolving right in front of her eyes.

"What happened?" she asked when he removed his hand and hurriedly took notes. He looked compassionate but moved somewhat automatically, his compassion a trained and contained expression. She didn't know how to feel about that specific kind of coolness.

"You suffered a serious brain injury. Some paralysis should be expected, even considering the express first aid you received. We will work on rehabilitation, of course."

"So I will get back to the way I was before?" Elle fired, impatient.

"We can't know for sure, ma'am. For now, try to get as much rest as possible. You're still in the very early stages of recovery." He smiled encouragingly and left the room.

The nurse quickly followed, having shown Elle the way to call if she were in need of anything and supplying her with a set of new water bottles. Having learned about her state, all tiredness escaped Elle's body. She felt nervous and on edge, uncertain about her professional future, and most of all, lost. She tried remembering what had led to the accident but couldn't remember anything besides an abysmal feeling of stress. Must have been before she was hit by the debris. She grew scared that it was her own fault, that due to her being distracted, she'd made a mistake, and out of politeness, none of the visitors had told her. Fear nested itself in her stomach and sat there until her thoughts were interrupted by her phone ringing on the nightstand. Its vibrations were bringing it closer and closer to the edge of the stand, so finally, Elle reached to pick it up.

"Yes?" she said, still completely unused to the weak sound of her voice.

"Elle?" Captain Hunter, of all people, Elle was definitely not expecting it to be her on the phone. "How are you feeling?"

"Uhm... Well, difficult to say." Elle felt unprepared to describe her state, though she realized she'd have to endure many such conversations in the following weeks. "It's not a great feeling to be lying here while all of you are still facing whatever's left of the earthquake's destruction. How is it going, by the way?"

"Hmm... We managed to rescue many people from the unfortunate shopping center. You know the one. Don't beat yourself up. You know it's ridiculous to feel guilty. We're going to manage. We only need you to take your time healing, and maybe also have a good chat with Maya."

"How do you all know Maya?" Elle could swear she heard Hunter smirk while saying that last part. She had no idea what could have happened during those few days she was unconscious.

"We met her in the hospital. She was the one who sewed you up, by the way."

"What?" Elle could believe what she was hearing.

"Yeah, was I not supposed to tell you that? She was there, carried you on the stretchers and did surgery on you in the ambulance. Rode with you all the way, too. She really cares about you, so don't fuck it up, huh?"

"Well... Thanks for telling me." Her voice grew a little bit stronger with every word, as if her vocal cords were getting newly used to speaking. "And how's the.. The girl's family?"

"Oh." Hunter quieted down herself now, "Maria's? She had a beautiful funeral. Of course her family is devastated, but they knew the risk that comes with the job, Elle."

"Hmm." Elle wanted desperately to open up to Hunter about the memory of the day and the guilt that followed. It was still hiding in a corner of her mind and still weighed heavy. She wanted to connect with someone who'd been there, too, and ask how Hunter was managing the feeling herself. Elle took a deep breath, then asked, "How are you feeling about it, Hallie?"

Hunter stayed quiet for a while. Elle could only hear the occasional sounds of breathing on the line. She enjoyed this wordless moment between them, acknowledging the heavy subject lying in between them, connecting their minds with a net of grief, of something unresolved that quietly knew its place in their conversation. When Hallie spoke, her voice was slightly raspy, more vulnerable than Elle had ever heard her be before.

"I've always known the risks of this job. For a long time, I thought having a family of my own would be impossible due to the nature of my profession. I took care of new recruits, I drilled into them the risks and importance of attention to detail and communication, all that so that they wouldn't go in and get themselves killed." She paused, drawing in a long breath before continuing. "I knew all that, Elle. And still—the day Maria fell, it felt as if some door suddenly opened and sucked me in with no way back. It was a shock to all of us, and there is no shame in your grief. I'd say it's actually quite expected."

Elle nodded pensively, grateful for each word that soothed her like dripping honey. There was no rush or impatience in Hunter's voice, and she realized this might had been what she needed all along.

"I think I needed to speak to you, specifically, about this. You know, because you were there, too. I feel like even though others mean well, talking to them doesn't make me feel at ease the same way talking to you does."

"That's understandable," Hunter replied.

"I still...I feel guilty about that. Not stopping it from happening, and now surviving even though the chances were slim." Elle wanted to put the raw feeling into some delicate words, wrap the soreness of it in wrapping paper and gift it to Hunter, hoping she'd unpack the burning sensation herself.

"That's a natural feeling. If I'm being honest with you, I feel it, too, every day since the accident." She paused. "But there's nothing we can do about it now, Elle, and pondering what ifs won't change the situation. We just need to march onward, help others, teach them better, be more attentive, and allow ourselves to grieve in private. You'll have a lot of time to process everything now. From what I hear, you're not getting out any time soon."

Elle was infinitely grateful for the smooth subject change. She'd received all the reassurance she could ask for and felt a bit more comfortable with her still raw emotions. Then she looked at her legs, resigned.

"I don't know what will happen to me. I have no feeling in my legs," she said, sighing.

"Fuck."

"Yeah. They're talking about rehabilitation, though, and that it's difficult to say how well I'll recover just yet. So maybe it's not going to be that bad..." Elle said with a bit more hope in her tone than what she really felt.

"Well, fingers crossed. You know we've all got your back at the station, Elle. I need to get going now, and I'm sure you need some sleep, too, but if you ever need anything from us, then you know who to call."

Hanging up, Elle felt the need to process all the information she'd learned from Hunter. The fact that it was Maya who'd saved her life weighed heavily on her, knowing how difficult it must have been like to operate on someone she knew, and Elle's head, no less. She craved the need to talk to her but felt too depleted by all the day's encounters to pick up the phone again. Her body felt leaden, craving sleep.

Her eyes began closing, but something stopped her from falling asleep just yet. Through the remaining slits of her vision, she saw a newspaper lying on the nightstand. Curious, Elle reached for it and studied the first page.

Another firefighter gravely injured following the tragic death of firefighter Maria Smith!

"Oh look, Mom, I've made it into the newspapers," Elle muttered to herself.

The piece had a sensationalist tone, full of exclamation marks and speculative writing. The journalist tried guessing Elle's injuries but clearly didn't have any reliable sources. On the left was a picture of Maria's funeral. Elle felt strange, being lumped together with Maria on the same page. She supposed she'd been close to death, but having survived, she didn't feel the actual danger that had loomed over her before. Everything had happened to her while she was unconscious from start to finish, and she felt as if the near deadness of it had eluded her completely. She hadn't experienced any fear for her life, or at least didn't remember.

When she settled in her bed once more readying herself to sleep, the memories of her and Maya following Maria's death came to her mind. She remembered how gentle Maya was, how effortlessly caring. She hoped this would still be the case when they saw each other again. She knew she'd have to apologize once and for all, make a blank slate for both of them to rewrite their story together. The right words would have to come to her somehow so Maya would know how much she cared about her.

Thinking this through, her eyes began closing, this time finally taking her away into the soft sheets of sleep. This time she had no dreams, no memories playing in her head. Her body was thrown into a restorative kind of rest, every tissue fighting to bring her back together.

16

MAYA

After the swift phone conversation with Ramirez, Maya felt as if her whole body was being constantly pinched by needles, no matter whether she sat, stood, walked around, or worked. And she had to work. The constant income of ambulances overflowing with patients put oceans of work on her and her colleagues' backs, tens of hours overtime, painkillers, black coffees, energy drinks, and Ubers home. She felt desperate to see Elle, yet she had to wait until the end of her never-ending shift. She had to think of her patients. She had to remain attentive during surgery. Often, she felt inhuman, above-human in some sense, existing only within the framework of her work. But that had to be broken for Elle.

Finally, at the fringes of dawn, she was free to go. Her limbs and back felt incredibly sore, but the air was fresh, the kind of freshness that only late summer at dawn can provide. She couldn't go to Elle at this hour, naturally, yet she couldn't force herself to go home to sleep, either, afraid she'd oversleep and miss the visiting hours window. She decided to drive to a cafe and wait there, perhaps pick up a book on her way, even though she knew very well she'd have no patience or focus for reading.

She drove her car for the first time in days, feeling strangely at peace, knowing what to do. She'd make sure Elle got the best care, the best advice, the best rehabilitation team. This was one advantage of being a doctor she'd never let go of—she always knew what was best for her family, or at least had the tools to learn it quickly.

Was Elle her family again? Maya didn't want to ponder the question before having the chance to talk to her.

She knew a bakery-coffee shop open from 6 a.m. and directed her car there. It was usually full of businesspeople readying themselves for a work-related flight or hopeless cases of partying all night and looking for a place to sit with a coffee in the morning. She liked observing them, the people who'd clearly pulled an all-nighter but definitely not for work-related reasons. Their lives seemed so strangely separated from hers, seemed so completely frivolous and alien. Even in med school, she could never afford to party like that. Some of the teenagers, or people in their early twenties, sat coupled, ostentatiously in love. Sipping from the same cup, sneaking each other little kisses. For the first time in years, however, Maya didn't feel jaded about seeing them. There was no tinge of jealousy, only a touch of warmth of recognition. She smiled to herself, ordering a lavender latte.

Sitting down with her drink, Maya checked the time. 6:36 a.m. She felt like risking it and calling Colin. Sometimes he had to be up at this hour, so perhaps she could catch him brushing his teeth or buttoning his shirt. The steady beeping on the line made her feel drowsy for a moment, the tiring night finally laying its claim on her mind, but Colin's voice quickly brought her back on track.

"What's up?" he said with a barely concealed yawn.

"I hoped you'd have a second to talk, maybe?" She let her voice take its natural route instead of pretending she wasn't tired, that she wasn't worried and overwhelmed.

"What happened? Are you all right?"

"The whole situation is weighing a bit heavy on me, you know. Elle being in a hospital and me still having to work instead of being by her side. It feels wrong." She let out a quiet sigh, passively watching two sleepless teenagers make out in a quiet corner. Noticing she was staring, she quickly turned her gaze away. "What do you think?"

"I think you should take a break from work and be with Elle, since you'd gotten so close to each other. She literally almost died."

"I can't just *take a break from work*. We're still dealing with the earthquake's aftermath, and the hospital is the fullest it has ever been. Do you think I can just--"

"Do you not have any days of paid leave left?" He interrupted her spiraling.

"I do, but--"

"Well then, what's the problem? Stop making excuses for yourself and commit to the idea of you two being seriously together. Help her. One surgeon less for two days won't change the world," Colin said a bit overconfidently, but Maya had to admit he had a point.

"You're right. You're right. I don't want to leave my team all alone, but two days won't hurt."

"There you go."

"How's Alexei doing? I'm sorry I haven't been to visit for so long." Maya felt a pang of guilt, thinking of her nephew. Recently her life had been so hectic that she'd made no time to check in on him.

"Ah don't worry. He's doing surprisingly great, just like you said he would. He's back in school, recovered in record time. Thanks to you, Maya."

"If it wouldn't have been me, it would have been someone else. You know that. But I'm really happy to hear that he's back to his life."

After exchanging thoughts on their parents' house, and Colin listing how the renovation had been going, he reminded Maya that he had to get to work. Hastily, they said their goodbyes, and now she was sitting with a cold latte in her hand, having forgotten to drink it while talking to Colin. Her watch read 7:40 a.m. They'd been talking for an hour. She gulped down the rest of her coffee, tasting the condensed lavender syrup at the bottom, then got up and headed to her car. It was time. She would finally get to see Elle, and if everything went well, she'd get to have an important conversation with her.

The traffic was light, and she felt as if her car soared through the newly laid out lanes. The city'd had to fix the roads cracked open by the earthquake, and the fresh, smooth asphalt felt heavenly beneath the wheels of the car. No bumps on the road, no harsh friction.

When she arrived at the hospital, a chilling sensation ran down her back. She remembered all too vividly carrying Elle inside the hall, waiting and waiting on the visitors' couch, making her spine sore and her legs itchy for movement. She'd have to wait now, too. The visiting window would open within a half an hour, and she once again had to let her body rest against one of the uncomfortable couches. The magazines laid out for the visitors talked about medicine, fashion, and childcare. There were some newspapers lying around, too, but she didn't feel like diving into the abyss of descriptions of suffering all around the city. She really wished the earthquake could leave her mind already, everyone's minds, that they could carry on with their lives as before. Unfortunately, that wouldn't be the case for long months to come.

"Dr Monroe?" A nurse called her into Elle's room, and Maya shakily followed.

The room had the characteristic atmosphere of hospital convalescence. The blinds were pulled down on the windows, and water bottles lay around the bed and on the nightstand. But Maya's eyes quickly landed on Elle. Her chest rose and fell with the peaceful rhythm of sleep, so vulnerable and innocent that Maya felt like kissing Elle's forehead. She sat down on a chair set against one of the walls, instructed by the nurse to wait until Elle would wake up. Elle's eyes moved frantically from left to right below her eyelids, meaning she was in a REM state.

Maya couldn't help but look at her and wonder, trying to divine what the dreams could be about. She rarely remembered her own dreams. Her sleep was either too short and weak, or she had to get up and get going too quickly to remember. The dreams would evaporate from her head as soon as she'd left the house. But lying in a hospital bed all day, she thought, one must spend a lot of time with one's dreams and memories.

After a long while of sitting around reading the

leftover newspapers and thinking of what she'd like to say – Elle woke up. Her eyes scanned the room, and upon finding Maya, her lips spread in a smile so warm Maya couldn't help but blush.

"Hello," she said softly.

"Hello." Elle's voice sounded a little raspy, but Maya could see that she was happy to see her. "Come here," she spread her arms, inviting Maya in for a hug.

She didn't have to repeat herself. Not even a second passed before Maya was in her arms, barely containing tears of relief. "I was so, so worried about you," she whispered.

Elle laid a gentle kiss on her cheek. "I know. They told me you brought me here when I was unconscious."

Maya looked at her, surprised. "Who told you that?"

"It doesn't matter." Elle smiled, shaking her head. She brought Maya's face closer to her own, and they shared a slow, tender kiss.

Maya felt a great need to hold Elle, feel her body close and alive, breathing, warm, and moving. She never wanted to stop kissing her, or be in her arms, but she knew they'd have to wait for that, that she couldn't tire Elle too much.

Gently, she pulled away, pressing one last kiss on Elle's face.

"How are you feeling?" She involuntarily scanned the monitors next to Elle's bed, looking at the way they changed with her being awake, studying the activity of her body in detail. But she wanted to be present, to hear Elle's voice and drown in it.

"Well, let's begin by saying what I am not feeling. I can't feel my legs."

Maya looked at her seriously. "So I've heard," she said. She knew there was a chance for recovery, however, and knew they'd work hard to make it happen. "But you have a chance at recovery."

Elle nodded. Maya could see she was scared of the reality in which she wouldn't be able to walk and would have to change her career. She didn't press. She knew Elle didn't like to talk about her feelings, and it wasn't necessary at this moment.

"I want you to know I'll be there for you every step of the way," Maya said carefully. "If you want me to be, of course."

Elle turned her head away, though she took Maya's hand. "Of course. I think we need to talk about some things first, though. I need to tell you some things, at least."

"I'm listening." Maya's heartbeat jumped into her throat. Was Elle breaking up with her? She didn't like the serious tone of Elle's voice, nor the way she wouldn't look into Maya's eyes, turning her head away. She kept her hand in Elle's, hoping she couldn't feel her rising heartbeat. Elle remained quiet, making her even more nervous. "What is it, Elle?"

"It's... It's difficult for me," Elle turned her head to finally look at Maya. She took a deep breath in, then began. "I owe you a true apology, first of all. You know that apologizing doesn't come easily to me. Actually, I think this will be the first time in my life when I have to do it from the bottom of my heart without being a coward. But I hope you'll be patient with me."

Maya nodded, unable to speak due to the growing tightness in her throat. Elle understood.

"Thank you. I've been reflecting on my past a lot the past few days, and as you know, working on my feelings for the past few months. But here in the hospital, a lot of memories came to my mind, some that I'd forgotten, some I'd hidden away on purpose. But lying here all on my own, it was impossible not to confront certain things." She paused, Maya could see that saying these things took a lot of effort. "I thought about the way things went down between us, and the way I behaved."

She took time to look deep into Maya's eyes before saying, "I behaved very selfishly a lot of the time, and never really faced the way I betrayed you back then. I need you to know, I regret it, truly regret it, to this day, and I'm sorry for what I've done. Being with you was the best time of my life. Being with you now is invigorating and dear to me. I've never felt about another woman the way I feel about you, not in all these years. Maybe it's different for you. Maybe you've known more intense love. But for me, it's always been you. That's the way I feel, and that's what I needed to say."

Having said everything, she carefully took her hand away, giving Maya time to think. Maya stood in complete awe. Everything she'd needed to hear from Elle, everything that was on her mind, had just been put into words and offered to her on a platter. She scrambled to put together a well-thought response, something that would match Elle's intensity, but her lungs seemed in a horrible hurry and her eyes welled with tears, blurring everything and making her overwhelmed with positive emotions.

"Elle, give me a moment, I'm sorry, I--" Maya struggled to put the words together. "I'm really glad to hear this. I'm so relieved."

Elle smiled. "Do you accept my apology?"

"Yes! Yes, Darling, I do." Maya took Elle's hands this time, but that wasn't enough, so she leaned in and gave her a kiss. What was supposed to be a short kiss quickly turned into a long, tongue-laced one, and they had to remember at the end of the day, they were in a hospital.

"I've been waiting to put this behind us for so long," she added, still dizzy from the kiss.

"And you understand that I'd never do this to you again?"

"I... I trust you, Elle." Maya nodded. Her chest was fluttering with excitement, and an overwhelming feeling of hope nested safely in her mind. "So would you... Would you like to officially get back together?"

"A million times *yes*. Though I don't want you to think I apologized only to get back together. If you'd prefer to stay friends, or whatever else, I'll be... I'll be in pain, but I'll understand."

"Don't be silly." Maya shook her head. "That was the most heartfelt apology I've ever received. I would love for us to get back together. I think that the past few weeks have shown me that more than anything." She looked aside for a moment, flustered. "Besides, I wanted to tell you that you're not alone in feeling that what we had—have—is special. I also haven't felt for anyone what I feel for you, Elle."

Having heard that, Elle seemed more relaxed. The familiar smile crept up her lips, and she leaned in to whisper something. "Let's celebrate."

"What do you mean by that? Aren't we celebrating?" Maya looked at her, not understanding. Elle looked mischievous, her eyes sparkling like a little kid's. "Elle?"

"Do you think you could smuggle in a drink?" She winked.

"Elle, this is a hospital, and you had a grave brain injury. Do you think that as a doctor, I'd actually bring in alcohol?" Maya laughed at the idea, messing with Elle's hair. "You can survive without it."

"Come on, I'm bored to death here. I want to celebrate with you. I hope you can stay for some time longer," she explained innocently.

"I can bring you non-alcoholic champagne and stay overnight. How about that?" Maya stood up from the edge of the bed where she'd been sitting.

"That's perfect." Elle nodded. "But what do you mean? Aren't you working?"

"I took some time off," Maya explained. "Two days to actually spend time with you and make it a little less boring here, hopefully." She looked around. "The white color everywhere is truly dreadful, huh?"

"I'm actually going insane because of it. I don't think I'll be able to look at anything white for the rest of my life." They laughed a little, enjoying this relaxed atmosphere after their tense confessions. "If we move in together, nothing can be white, Maya."

"All right, we'll see about that. I'm not giving up my flat. I just bought it."

"I have a house, though."

"How about we have this conversation some other time?" Maya leaned in to give Elle another kiss and was warmly received by her lips. "I'll go and get that wine."

Once she was back, they opened the bottle and pretended as if it were really making them tipsy, getting more and more creative in their ways to imitate a state of drunkenness. They also made use of the hospital's games, quickly abandoning sophisticated pursuits like chess or even checkers in favor of the games clearly meant for families with little children.

They got so loud at times that a nurse had to come in, reminding them to respect the other patients and be quiet.

"I feel like a little child," Maya said, choking down a laugh. She couldn't remember a time when she'd laughed this much. "I should know better. I'm a doctor."

"They'll get over it." Elle tucked Maya's hair behind her ear. "You won't get over this, however." And she ate Maya's last hippopotamus, making her lose the game.

"Fuck you." Maya jokingly got up to go.

"We can play again. I'll go easy on you." Elle opened it again, making space on the bed.

After some time, Elle started getting visibly sleepy. Maya couldn't help thinking it was quite cute, the way she would uncontrollably yawn and let her eyelids fall almost all the way down her drowsy eyes.

"Would you like to go to sleep?" Maya suggested, following another series of very infectious yawns.

"Come on, I'm not a toddler," Elle said in a mock-offended tone.

"Let me rephrase. I'd like to go to sleep," Maya corrected herself. "I was awake the whole previous night."

"Oh." Elle nodded. "Sure, then. Are you taking *the couch*?" She pointed to the very uncomfortably looking chair.

"With pleasure." Maya sighed. "I'll get myself some pillows and a blanket. Will you wait for me?"

"Very funny."

But Elle did not wait, in fact. Once Maya was back after asking the irritated nurse for pillows, she saw her darling had already drifted off somewhere far away in the thick coat of deep sleep. She quietly settled herself in the chair, perplexed as to where to put her legs so as not to look too ridiculous, but also to be able to fall asleep, at least for a moment. The blanket was a bit scratchy and quite warm, but she couldn't be happier. She was back with Elle without compromising her boundaries, without making a fool out of herself. She was back with Elle on her own terms, having heard one of the most beautiful apologies of her life. Sincere and made with effort. From time to time glancing at sleeping Elle, she soon drifted off herself, unaware of how painful her back would be the next day.

"Elle, Darling." she delicately shook Elle's arm, sorry to have to wake her up, but also incredibly excited. She touched her arm again, "Elle?"

"Maybe we should wait, you know, she seems deep asleep," Colin suggested, shifting his weight from one foot onto another, visibly nervous.

"Perhaps," Maya looked at Elle regretfully. "But you'll have to go soon. I really wanted you two to talk to each other again." she smiled.

"Who is it?" Elle's voice interrupted their conversation. She stirred in her bed without opening her eyes, her voice still carrying in it little grains of sleep. She sighed, then prepared to fall asleep again, tucking herself into the sheets.

"Elle?" Maya said gently. "Colin came to visit."

Elle opened her eyes this time. She looked Colin up and down, and her face lit up. "Colin! Come here, you, I need a hug," she said, almost laughing.

"We haven't seen each other for so long," Colin came up to hug her, awkwardly careful, as if not knowing whether he would break anything. Maya always thought it endearing the way he behaved in hospitals, walking on eggshells. "I was always rooting for you two to get back together," he half-whispered.

"Hey! That's not a supportive thing to say," Maya reprimanded him, joining in for the hug.

She felt completely at peace, having both Elle and Colin with her again, felt ready to give Elle all of her support in the process of rehabilitation. She also felt ready to face work again, knowing she always had Elle to lean upon and get back to. They finally released each other, beyond happy from the reunion.

"Tell me everything," Elle said first. "How's it going? What happened after your wedding? That's when I stopped following along." Maya could see that she was hungry for details and felt glad that she could bring the two back together.

Back when Maya and Elle were dating, Elle had gotten along with Colin very well. Soon, Maya began catching them hanging out without her when she'd had to stay at med school until late, and their friendship had quickly blossomed. Then, Colin went away to study, and the breakup between Maya and Elle obviously kept Elle and Colin further apart. Seeing their friendship rekindle felt good, though a bit nostalgic for Maya, reminiscent of a long-gone period of their lives.

"Well, my son Alexei is all grown now. You should definitely meet him, You'll get along with each other very well, I'm sure."

"I'd love to." Elle nodded vigorously. "I remember him as a little toddler."

"Has Maya told you?" Colin looked toward Maya in a way of silent question. "Does Elle know?"

Maya shook her head. "I don't think so."

"Oh, some time ago, Alexei's school bus was involved in an accident, and he was saved by no one else than Maya herself." He nodded. "I can't imagine how terrifying it must have been, to operate on someone you know."

"Yes, she tends to do that a lot, doesn't she?" Elle winked at Maya but didn't say anything else about being saved. "She's a really good surgeon, and I can't stop being proud of her," she said to Colin as if Maya weren't in the room with them.

"All right, stop this. It's just my job," Maya protested. "You don't like people going up to you saying you're a hero and all that either, do you, now."

"Oh, I love it." Elle laughed. "I'm a narcissist. Didn't you know?"

She and Colin laughed. Maya could only look

at them and feel her chest grow warm. "We're the stereotype, Elle," she said after a while. "We're the gay aunts."

"Wouldn't prefer to be anything else," Elle said to her warmly.

"Wouldn't you..?" Maya asked, but the question escaped Elle's attention.

Sometimes she caught herself imagining scenarios she wouldn't feel brave enough to ask Elle about, definitely not so early on in their newly renewed relationship. But the image of her, Elle, and a child sometimes did creep up in her mind. It was a distant and abstract idea, and yet. She was afraid Elle would never consider it seriously, so she preferred to think of it as something abstract and extravagant, a fancy she wouldn't ever consider bringing into reality. She shook her head, wanting to be present in the moment.

"Elle, I hope you'll come around sometime for a barbeque or something. Are you still good with a grill?" Colin asked.

"Well, as soon as I can walk," Elle replied jokingly, though Maya could see the thought cut through her joy and reminded her of her miserable state of affairs.

"Shit, I'm sorry, I forgot." Colin scratched his

head awkwardly. "I'm sure you'll recover, though. Your care will be under the watchful eye of Maya, and she won't let anyone bullshit you."

"Then you don't bullshit me and say things that may not come true." Elle looked at him seriously. "I'm dying to meet Alexei, though. As soon as I'm out of here, we should plan something together. And yes, I am *amazing* when it comes to grilling." Her expression softened with a playful smile.

Once Colin and Elle said their goodbyes, Maya left to walk him out of the hospital.

"I'm glad you two are still getting along great," she said proudly.

"Yeah, she hadn't changed at all." He smiled. "Really glad you guys are back together. You seem to fit each other pretty well."

"You're right, as always."

Outside the door a chilly morning awaited them. Lazy clouds spread all over the bright blue sky, and Maya thought of the approaching autumn. She couldn't wait to see it. Autumn in Phoenix Ridge was the most beautiful season with its golden leaves carpet-like decorating the streets, the autumn sun shining through the bare branches of trees. She couldn't wait to experience it again with Elle by her side, doing all the nauseatingly couplish things together in their spare time.

Maya and Colin hugged each other goodbye and he was off, looking for his car, having forgotten where he parked it again. She watched him walk around the lot, lovingly amused. He never remembered where he'd left his car. Sometimes, she thought, people don't change and don't have to.

Going back inside the hospital, she knew she'd soon have to say goodbye to Elle and was trying to push the moment as far away in her thoughts as possible. She couldn't agree with Colin regarding Elle – Elle had changed, for the better. She was more open to talk about her feelings with Maya, more open to being vulnerable with her than when they'd been together before. That made her feel proud. Elle was ready to work on herself and change for Maya, putting in real effort to be with her.

"Hello again." She walked into the room where Elle was waiting. "How are you feeling? Do you need anything?"

Elle didn't look good. Her eyes glanced around nervously and she appeared to be glistening with sweat. Maya stopped at the threshold, worried.

"I feel stressed about something, like—really stressed. Do you feel as if I've forgotten something important?" She looked at Maya. "My chest is tingling."

Maya came up closer, wanting to comfort Elle. Brain injuries could cause random waves of stress, and she knew how frustrating it would be for Elle to learn she was feeling this way for no real reason. She sat on the edge of the bed, taking Elle's hand.

"Everything is all right. You didn't forget anything." She traced Elle's knuckles with her fingers. "You may start feeling this way sometimes without any actual reason. I mean, there's a reason, but it's a physical one. It's from your injury, and it can fuck with you like that from time to time."

Elle tried breathing in, but her breath seemed to crumble somewhere on the way to her lungs. She closed her eyes. "And what can I do when this happens?"

"Anything you normally would when you're stressed. Anything that will help you relax." Maya kept talking in a gentle voice. "You can also ask the nurse for a sedative. They can give you that."

"Hmm…" Elle looked at her. "In a moment, maybe. Can I kiss you?"

Maya's lips spread into a little smile. "Is that what you do when you're stressed?"

"Always," Elle said, pulling her in for a kiss.

Their lips met tenderly, slowly exploring each other, taking their time to savor the kiss. Maya could feel Elle relax a little, and she put one hand on Elle's neck, wanting to draw her in closer. They remained this way for a while, simply breathing in each other's existence, forgetting again that they were in a hospital.

"Baby, we're forgetting ourselves again." Maya slowly pulled away, leaving a kiss on Elle's forehead.

"Only you can call me Baby without it sounding strange, do you know that?"

"Well," Maya smiled mischievously. "I'll make sure to make use of the privilege."

They spent the hospital breakfast together, then kept prolonging the moment of parting ways. Their time together felt pleasantly sticky, like honey during summer, glistening in the sun and making children's fingers stick to each other. Maya felt powerless to drag her limbs away from the hospital, felt as if she could make the minutes last longer if only she tried.

"Maya, you should get some actual rest before

you go back to work, you know," Elle kept saying while messing with Maya's hair. "I'll be worried about you otherwise."

"I'll go." She sighed. "I just don't want to leave you again, I've missed you so much, and you're finally awake."

"You'll visit me again soon." Elle lifted Maya's face to meet her eyes. "You will, right? You'll visit me very soon?"

"Of course." Maya took Elle's hands in her own. "And make sure to keep me updated on your treatment. Run everything by me, okay?"

Elle grunted. Maya knew she felt babied by the request.

"Okay?" she repeated. "It's important, I want you to get an opinion from as many specialists as you can, and that includes me."

"Yeah I guess," Elle said, but then she made an effort to add, "Thank you. You're being helpful, I know. Thank you."

Maya kissed her forehead again, delighting in being able to do so. She now had the forehead kissing license back indeterminably. That made her want to giggle and do it all over again.

"I'm so happy to be with you," she confessed, prolonging the moment on Elle's bed.

"I'm happy to be with you, too. Hopefully I'll be with you out of this hospital soon. Now go! Pack your things, Maya," she laughed, "you need to take care of yourself, too."

Maya nodded, beginning to pack her stuff. Over the course of the last twenty hours she'd managed to get everything tangled with Elle's things, abandoned in various places around the bed. It made her happy to be so comfortable with Elle as to show her messiness, let her things fall and be lost. She knew they'd find them again, together.

Having packed everything, it was time for her to go. She stood next to the bed, unable to say goodbye.

"We'll see each other again soon," she said, reassuring herself more than Elle.

"We have to." Elle nodded. "But you also have to take care of our city. I can wait for a little while."

"All right. All right. Don't be trite." Maya laughed. "But you're right. There's still so much to do... Hopefully we'll put this whole earthquake avalanche of tragedy behind us soon."

"Hopefully," Elle agreed.

They shared an overly long goodbye hug, then Maya was finally on her way. She felt upset to have to leave Elle, her heart breaking on her way to the car, but the premise of falling asleep in her bed seemed irresistibly delicious to her. For too many nights she had skipped or foregone sleep or slept in the hospital chair, and now the idea of her tailored mattress and light, summer duvet that would envelop her with softness called.

On the way, she thought about calling her parents under the pretext of checking in on the progress of their building renovations, of course, but really for some other, unclear to her reason. She sometimes had the impulse to talk to them in moments of joy or achievement, as if to say: *Look! The life you brought into the world is not so bad at all.* Perhaps it was from some blend of gratefulness and desire to share her joy. How strange, she thought, to have grown estranged from those who brought her here in the first place, from those who'd given her the opportunity to experience all the richness of life. But then, maybe the ones who shared these joys and the richness of it mattered most.

She yawned, entering her apartment. Its large windows let in thick rays of sunlight, and she thought of the way she'd spend the day before going to sleep early. She couldn't allow herself to sleep through the day unless she wanted her circadian rhythm to be completely ruined. The sun was so tempting, she decided to go for a stroll in the nearby park. Its alleys were always overflowing with people, and she liked to watch them. Glance here then there, see grandmas pushing baby strollers with their grandchildren, young couples walking their dogs, or little kids learning to walk, chuckling and falling into their parents' arms.

Yes, she would go to the park, feel the sunlight soak her skin and remember that everything between her and Elle would be good from now on, her injury their only pressing obstacle. She set her bag down and went to change into fresh clothes. Even at the brink of autumn, she felt springful, reborn in the city of her past. She thought about places that could change skin like a serpent, wriggle out of the scales of memories and inhabit something new, some hopeful corners of the future where there was still space for things to come.

She made herself green tea before leaving, watching the steam evaporate toward her ceiling. Would she need to let go of her place to live with Elle? She didn't want to be the one making sacrifices again. She promised herself that she'd think the matter through and let Elle know her preference, without shaming or disregarding her own opinions. She knew Elle would take it, striving to figure out something to suit them both. She took long sips of the tea, feeling it warm her stomach. Then she set the empty cup down and went out to taste the sun.

17

ELLE

The pain soared through her limbs, carrying her mind somewhere far and bright, unreal from the intensity of the sensations. She felt like crying, but no tears came to her eyes. She was only able to whisper "Fuck, fuck, fuck," but her physiotherapist was used to her vulgarities by that point. Elle appreciated her steel-like nerves and no-bullshit approach, hiding behind friendly and helpful interactions.

"You're doing great, Elle." Michelle held her calves in her hands. "Just a little bit more. You've got it! There you go!"

"You're a fucking sadist, Michelle. You're a sadist," Elle said through her clenched teeth as she tried as hard as she could to move the other leg.

Her body felt stiff and unused to movement from weeks of lying in the hospital bed.

"Maybe, but at least I'm getting you results," Michelle said good-naturedly. "Okay, let's take a break."

For the past few weeks, Elle had been giving her best at the physiotherapy sessions. When the doctors let her know that there was a glimpse of hope that she could walk again, Elle put every bit of strength toward achieving that goal. Her sessions were exhausting and long, but the work was paying off. She could walk a few steps, even though her brain was screaming at her not to, even though her legs felt on fire. Michelle was Maya's colleague and practically the best physiotherapist in the city. She often pushed Elle to her utmost limits, but she always knew when to stop. Their relationship grew strong with time, and Elle was increasingly able to trust Michelle's judgment.

"Should we call it a day, then?" Elle said, feeling like a sweaty, panting mess.

"I think so. How are you feeling?" Michelle patted Elle's back, gathering up her things.

Elle got into her wheelchair, wiping her face. "Sweaty."

"That's good! It's like working out. The more

effort you put in, the more you'll get out of it. You're making real progress, Elle."

"All thanks to you," she said simply.

Chatting, they went out of the clinic. Elle was still getting used to being in a wheelchair. The world around her looked very different from its perspective, and going through the streets in a sitting position still often caught her off guard. She couldn't drive, which grieved her tremendously, and had to order Ubers that would be accessible to her, which often meant waiting longer than usual. Because of all the obstacles, she didn't like going out alone. Sometimes a bunch of her friends would come visit and go out with her. She had to be careful not to drink and choose venues that would be wheelchair accessible. The inability to walk opened her eyes to many issues she wouldn't have thought of otherwise. At first, her house hadn't been wheelchair accessible, so she and Maya had to install a ramp. She tried going upstairs on her own many times, but she'd get tired midway.

She felt strange about her legs being fully able to walk, only her brain not knowing how to use them. It was as if she'd gone back to being a baby again, unable to climb the stairs and having to rely on the help of others.

On the other hand, this experience had made her ask for help so many times that she'd finally had to learn to accept it. She'd grown more comfortable with asking for help, even if she still disliked it tremendously and would rather suffer. Everything came to her little by little. Accepting help and being able to walk again, she knew she'd manage both. Especially having Maya by her side. Their relationship had flourished despite the workload Maya was under, and Elle appreciated every single moment they got to spend together, no matter how brief or sparse.

She got out of the van, thanked the driver, and rode up to her house. Strangely, ever since she'd come back from the hospital in a wheelchair, Mrs. Dumas had kept quiet around her. No bickering or unpleasantries, not a single thing muttered under her breath. Maybe she thought that at the end of the day firefighters did deserve the pay that they got.

If I were her I'd feel silly too, Elle thought.

Mrs. Dumas's kids also appeared more polite, and the entire situation made Elle laugh a little whenever she would see them getting back from work, mowing their lawn, or whatever other family activity they partook in while making sure the entire neighborhood saw them. Sometimes she felt sorry for Mrs. Dumas. Her husband was almost never to be found doing the work around the kids. It was always she alone.

Elle's house stood as empty as always. She was getting sick of the solitude of it, the space that wasn't shared with anyone. It felt wrong to have the entire house to herself. Unnecessarily grandiose. She thought of selling it, of suggesting Maya to move in together into something they'd build. To have a home, like a real adult couple. She couldn't wait to see Maya again and discuss it with her, do something about all this emptiness. She was supposed to visit in the evening, but the day stretched like warm caramel, early afternoon golden with mature sunrays.

Elle's phone rang.

"Yes, Captain Ramirez?" she said in an all too happy tone. She lived for these phone calls, learning how the brigade were doing, how big or small the progress was. She felt as if a part of her rested there at the station, though she couldn't get back to it.

"Hi, Rodriguez."

She heard the familiar voice and couldn't help smiling."

"How is your physiotherapy going?"

"It's going as fast as it can. Which is not very quickly." Elle sighed. "How is the team doing?"

"Everyone is missing you. Especially in the truck. You know O'Malley will never be as good a driver as you were." *Were* stung Elle's heart. She had to get used to her current life, but a part of her still yearned for the thrill of action.

"That's just obvious," she joked. "I hope I can get back someday."

"We all do." Ramirez paused for a moment, and Elle felt she had something on her mind. But Ramirez couldn't be rushed, and she knew that eventually she'd tell her. They rested quietly on the line for a while, enjoying the momentary comfortable silence.

"Listen," Ramirez began. "I have an offer for you."

"Oh really?" Elle's interest was piqued. "What is it?"

"I think it would do you good to do some work. I know you must be bored nuts right now, the only thing on your mind being rehabilitation. A woman can go insane this way, so I thought I'd talk to my superiors."

"And?"

"I have a job for you. A desk job, but it's all I can offer you for now. Once you're back on your feet, literally, you'll be able to join us again as a firefighter." Ramirez seemed proud of her suggestion, waiting excitedly for Elle to speak.

"A desk job? What kind of desk job?"

"Talent management. You would take care of newcomers to our brigade. Isn't that exciting? Judging people as a job? I think you'd be a perfect fit. On a more serious note, your achievements and years of experience would make you a valuable asset."

Elle sank into thought, never having considered working a desk job. She definitely had never considered hearing such an offer from Ramirez, but then, everything changes, and nothing should surprise her at this point.

"I'm grateful for the opportunity, Captain, I'll think about it. I'll let you know in the coming days. Is that all right?" She didn't sound convinced, but her words were sincere. She wanted to give it fair consideration, and she trusted Ramiez to know what she was saying.

"I know it's definitely a change from what you're used to. But sometimes changes are good, don't forget. You may learn something new, so give it some thought and don't hesitate to let me know. I'll support you either way."

"Thanks, Captain," Elle got slightly flustered, never knowing what to say in the face of such sincerity from Ramirez. Ever since her injury, their relationship had grown all the more affectionate.

Hanging up, Elle felt impatience creep up her back again. She felt such a strong urge to discuss everything with Maya, but there were still three hours left until she'd be able to get to Elle's place. She wanted to do something active while waiting.

From her kitchen cupboard, she took out her mother's old cookbook. Even though their relations had been sour for a long time, there was something tender about this spice-scented book containing the recipes Elle remembered from her childhood. She decided to prepare dinner for Maya.

Flipping through the book gave her a thousand ideas, and quickly, she became overwhelmed not knowing what to choose. An enchilada? A tostada? She remembered all the family dinners with ugly bowls and deliciously smelling dishes. Her own plates were beautiful, but she hadn't cooked in ages. She'd figure something out.

The plan she settled for was lobster enchilada as the main dish and vegetable quesadillas as the appetizer. She had to get to work, go shopping and start cooking, otherwise she'd run out of time. She got out of the house, grateful for a multicultural store right next to her.

The first part of her shopping went quickly—onions, peppers, jalapenos, corn, tomatoes, tomato paste, cilantro, beans, cheese, and guacamole. She had to get the lobster from somewhere, but she had no idea where that would be in her neighborhood. She could almost hear the disappointment in her mother's voice if she found out that Elle wasn't cooking for herself. Her mother had tried raising her daughter to be strong, but not strong the way men traditionally are – hiding their emotions and flexing physical strength. She wanted Elle to know how to take care of herself and not depend on anyone. She taught her how to cook, sew, and effortlessly find her way in the big city, all accompanied by Elle's childish complaining. Unfortunately for her mother, Elle's father had always been the stronger influence, his ways shaping his daughter more than her mother's teaching ever could.

She finally found a fish market. Going around in her wheelchair was still slowing her down significantly, though her technique was improving. She bought a big lobster, then questioned herself ever choosing a lobster dish.

Was she trying to show off? Probably.

Back home, she realized she had no time to waste. She had to put all of her half-forgotten cooking skills into the dinner, working tirelessly. She tried standing for most of the time, supporting herself against the kitchen counters, but whenever there was a need, she reached for her wheelchair or a stool. The kitchen was soon filled by the scents of her home cooking, and she began feeling very nostalgic. To share this with Maya would be a vulnerable gesture.

The enchiladas were safely nested in the oven when the doorbell rang. Elle wanted to run up to the door, but the cooking efforts had exhausted her, and she had to stay in the chair, rolling toward the door.

"Good evening." Maya smiled, walking in. Soon, she began sniffing in the fragrant air. "Elle, have you been cooking?" She turned towards Elle, surprised.

"I made us dinner," Elle said proudly. "What's more, I was actually standing almost the whole time."

"Are you kidding me? That's amazing news!" Maya leaned in for a quick kiss, and Elle could smell her beautiful flowery fragrance mingled with the remnants of a hospital scent.

"Yeah, let's sit down, though. The food is ready." she sat at one of the dining table chairs. Ever since the injury, she preferred to sit with Maya—at tables, on couches, or in bed. Then, she didn't feel strange being lower than her, the way she had to be when she sat in the wheelchair and Maya was standing.

Maya sat opposite her, clearly excited. Elle loved seeing her this way.

"I don't remember the last time you cooked for me, Elle. This is amazing, I'm starving. Tell me all about the food, though," she said, taking a quesadilla. "Bon Appetit!"

Elle also took one as she explained. "So actually, my mother left me her family cookbook. I don't know whether you remember that one time we tried making dessert from it, but we failed and never tried again."

"Hmm... I don't remember the book, exactly, but I surely remember some of our failed dessert attempts." Maya laughed, taking a bite. "This is so good. Thank you so much, Darling."

"I'll show you the book later, if you want. It's full of the things I ate as a child. It feels quite nostalgic to cook from it, you know."

"I'd love to see it!" Maya nodded excitedly, finishing her second quesadilla.

Elle smiled, remembering the lobster dish.

"Are you ready for the main dish?" she asked, carefully getting up and transferring onto her wheelchair. She thanked herself every day for making her kitchen large.

"Oh my god, of course." Maya got up, too. "Do you need any help?"

"No, no, it's fine," Elle said hurriedly, not wanting to be perceived as weak.

"Let me rephrase the question: Can I be around you in the kitchen so I don't feel useless?" Maya tilted her head, waiting for the answer.

"Sure. Let's go."

They had to wait twenty minutes for the enchiladas, and in the meantime, got busy with each other. They finally were out of the hospital, free to make out whenever they liked, for however long they liked. It felt fresh and liberating, youthful even. It was golden autumn outside, but their kisses felt like spring, blooming in unexpected places.

Maya loved to steal Elle's wheelchair and try rolling around the house. One time she bumped into the coffee table and knocked down a little ceramic vase, which scared her and then made her bump into a wall. It caused them both to laugh for long hours.

The timer rang.

"Let's get the food out," Elle exclaimed, realizing how hungry she felt. At first, she thought she wouldn't eat as much due to sitting in the chair all day, but she quickly learned that rolling it with her arms cost her as much effort if not more due to the new nature of the movement. "I'm starving, too."

"Let's get the food out!" Maya clapped. "You're my favorite chef."

"Yours and yours only, Baby." Elle laughed, getting the hot dish out.

They sat down again and began devouring the dish, feeling as if they possessed some secret key to happiness. Elle put on some jazz in the background and felt quite satisfied with herself. Full-bellied and well-humored, their conversation went in a more serious direction.

"I was thinking a lot today," Elle said. "About our future, my job, the house. I'd like to talk about a few things with you."

"You sound so mature." Maya laughed. "You're making me feel old, but maybe that's a good thing." The dim light from Elle's living room lamps was caught beautifully in Maya's hair, and for a moment she didn't respond, only sat with the beautiful sight of her girl.

"First, I wanted to say that I like the idea of moving in together. I'm sick of living on my own when I'm with the woman of my dreams. What would you say?"

"You know that I'd like that, too."

"And I know you don't want to let go of your apartment in favor of my place. I honestly don't want this house. I wanted to suggest that I sell it, for a time move into yours, and in the future we can build or find something larger together. Do you think you might consider that?" She put her hands together, curious to hear what Maya would say.

"I like that idea." Maya smiled. "We can

consider a house together later down the line," she said pensively.

"Great, I'll look into it, then, I can't wait to move out and be with you full time." Elle sighed with relief. Everything was going great, and the evening couldn't be any more perfect for her. "I also got a call from Ramirez today."

"What'd she say?" Maya asked, stacking the plates together to help clean up.

"She offered me a desk job."

"Oh?" Maya looked at her with careful curiosity. "What would it be, and what do you think about it?"

"Talent management. Basically handling recruitment, etc. I'm thinking about it." She looked down. "I probably won't be able to go back to my old job for years to come. I'd have to fully recover. And I need a job, so I'm thinking of taking it."

"That's a very wise idea. I think Ramirez really cares about you," Maya said while carrying the dishes to the kitchen.

"Stop cleaning up. You're a guest!" Elle shouted after her.

"I'm not a guest when I'm your partner. If you make the meal, I'll clean up. Don't worry." She went back to kiss Elle's head. "I think it'd be nice to at least see whether you like the job with the department. Maybe it'll surprise you."

"Maybe," Elle shrugged. "How is your work going?"

"Tiring. The insane inflow of patients finally stopped, and we're back to the usual. Should we watch something on TV?"

"Sure," Elle eagerly agreed.

They put on some French film, but neither of them were focused on it. Maya began sneakily kissing Elle's neck, and Elle retaliated, kissing her face.

"What are you doing, love?" she whispered, stroking Maya's back.

"Nothing," Maya said sweetly. "I'm just so happy to be here with you." She kissed Elle's lips, tracing them patiently with her mouth.

Soon, she was sitting on top of Elle, completely blocking the screen. Her hands were sliding up and down Elle's torso, now and then stroking her hard nipples.

"Nice movie," Elle joked, grabbing Maya's hips. "I missed you there."

"I know." Maya nodded. "We should've done this earlier."

Maya beautifully ground her hips into Elle, and Elle reached to take Maya's shirt off. She was thirsty to see her naked torso, her beautiful breasts moving in harmony with her body. Once the shirt was off, Maya's pinned hair fell down, cascading onto her shoulders and reaching down to her nipples in golden streaks.

"You're so beautiful," Elle whispered. "Have I ever told you that?" She rose to reach Maya's face and lay a kiss on her lips. Her tongue slipped in and out teasingly.

"Many times," Maya giggled, taking off her skirt. She was left in only her underwear.

"But have I *really* told you?" Elle teased, touching Maya's hardening nipples, driving her hands down to her panties. Her fingers began circling around Maya's clit through the thin fabric, taking her sweet time.

"Tell me again." Maya smirked, taking off Elle's shirt. "And I will tell you how beautiful *you* are. So beautiful I want to strip you naked and kiss your whole body."

"No one's stopping you," Elle said, unbuttoning her linen pants, in themselves hardly any barrier.

Through their fabric she could feel Maya's warm, naked thighs, grateful to be able to feel her legs to witness that. Her pants soon fell to the ground.

"Maya, I need to taste you on my tongue," Elle whispered into her ear, running her hands down Maya's back and reaching her butt. Maya began lowering her underwear, teasingly, sensually, obnoxiously slowly. Elle's mouth watered when the little piece of fabric finally fell to the floor.

Maya got on her knees and put herself to Elle's impatient mouth. They went slowly at first. Elle knew Maya liked riding her tongue best and was building up to that. Maya's thighs in her hands felt perfect, soft and smooth, exactly what she'd been craving. Soon, Maya began moaning, the sweet, quiet first moans Elle delighted in, and she kept going at their favorite pace, knowing exactly what to do and feeling blessed to know it. When her moans got louder, she sucked a little on Maya's clit and felt her come closer but wanted to prolong it so went back to sliding up and down, the moans forever growing louder.

When Maya came, they lay next to each other, panting. Their break didn't last for long, however, because soon Elle felt Maya's fingers around her pussy, tracing along her thighs, praying for them to open. Elle couldn't not listen. She loved being teased this way, and more than anything she loved showing how eager she was to get fucked. She knew very well that Maya got off on this as well, on seeing Elle squirm under her touch.

"The couch isn't the most comfortable, is it?" Maya said, her fingers dangerously close to Elle's opening.

"Mhmm, it's fine." Elle shrugged it off, impatient.

"Why don't we go to your bed?" Two of Maya's fingers slipped in, making lazy circles inside. "I think it'd be more comfortable, love."

"It's upstairs, though," Elle complained, not wanting to go through the difficulty of getting up there. She'd need to be helped and didn't want it to ruin the mood.

"Elle." Maya got closer to her, gently kissing her neck. "I'll always help you without question. You know that, Darling. I love you."

Elle stared at her, hearing her say *I love you* for the first time in seven years. Her heart stopped for a moment. She couldn't understand how casually it had escaped Maya's lips. She grabbed Maya's hands, laughing. "You can't say something like that while inside of me." She shook her head.

"I'm serious." Maya looked at her fingers, flustered. "Sorry about that. I want you to understand that I'm serious. I love you, Elle."

Elle pulled her closer, kissing her passionately.

"I love you, too," she finally felt ready to say, looking into Maya's eyes, confident in the strength of her feelings. They kissed again. "I love you a hundred times. Let's get ourselves upstairs." She nodded at the staircase.

"Yes." Maya got up, offering Elle support.

The trip upstairs went surprisingly smoothly. Elle could easily lean on Maya and was glad she had suggested it once they'd laid down on her bed. Its softness made them dizzy with pleasure, and the cool duvet felt salvatory against their heated skin.

Maya's fingers were strong and precise as usual, and she worked on Elle's body with no less craftsmanship than a sculptor creating a classical sculpture, attentive to each delicate detail and fold. Their bodies moved in delicious unison, and their panting was music to both of their ears. Once Elle came, they stayed in each other's arms for a while, breathing into each other's skin and enjoying their earthy tangle of chaotic hair and sweat-sticky limbs.

Without either noticing, night enveloped the windows all around the house, casting its soulful, shadowy spell on the atmosphere. Elle thought that the house wasn't that bad when Maya was in it, that indeed she could live in any house as long as they remained together.

"Should we put on some music?" she asked when the silence around them got a little bit too loud.

"Sure." Maya nodded. "What do you listen to these days?"

Elle got up, clutching the edge of her mirrored vanity. Her legs felt unruly, but she wanted to practice as much as she could. She knew it wasn't about the muscles being tired but her brain, and her brain seemed to her more plastic than her limbs.

"Some chill jazzy rap, mostly," she said, putting on her favorite playlist and falling back onto the bed, lying flat on her back, dizzy with the effort of standing.

"You know," Maya scootched closer to her, the beats of the music fuzzily enveloping her soft voice. "You shouldn't overwork yourself when you're recovering. You also need to allow yourself time to rest."

"But it's not my body that's actually tired. It's my brain. And I feel like I can bend it a little bit more to my will." Elle yawned.

"Your brain is a part of your body," Maya was quick to remind her. "And it can grow tired just like any muscle or limb. Rest will do you good from time to time."

"Whatever you say." Elle rolled onto her stomach, giving Maya the hundredth kiss of the evening. "You're the doctor."

They rolled around the bed, comfortable in each other's presence. Their confessions of love still occupied parts of Elle's mind, and it was still such a fresh thing. They began making out again, their tongues never tired of exploring each other's mouths, their embraces feeling as electric as ever.

"I want to fuck you again," Maya whispered into Elle's ear. "Can you take it?"

"*Can I take it?*" Elle laughed, "Baby, I'll take whatever you give me."

Excited, Maya left the bed. Waiting for her to get back, Elle knew what awaited her. She melted just at the thought. She felt Maya's hands on her ass cheek, diving in between her thighs from behind.

"Ah, look how wet you are. You can't wait, can you?" Maya smiled, her harness fully on. "I want to do something very intimate."

"Oh, yes?" Elle looked at her, waiting.

"Yes, I want to take you like this," Maya said, taking Elle in her arms.

They lay embracing each other closely, and Elle couldn't remember the last time they'd had sex in a true missionary position. Their faces close to each other felt like the most intimate experience on Earth.

"Do you like this?" Maya asked, pushing slightly stronger into Elle. Her hips were moving with a calm, steady rhythm, not wanting to take things too fast, too aggressively.

"I love it," Elle whispered, moaning quietly.

They moved entangled this way for what seemed like the sweetest kind of eternity, not the one that feels prolonged through nuisance, but the one that feels so sweet every second clings like syrup on a sticky summer day, melting into minutes like ice cream under the cruel rays of sun. Maya's skin glistened from sweat, and Elle wouldn't have it any other way than to be below her in that moment. Their breaths, tingly from the sweetness of non-alcoholic wine, mingled together, and Elle began craving a release.

"Make me come please," she moaned, getting wetter from hearing her own words exist in the space between her and Maya.

"As you wish," Maya whispered in response.

As her movement became increasingly sweet and aggressive, she reached to touch Elle simultaneously. Elle didn't know what pleased her more, the touch itself, or the feeling of Maya's hand knowing her every corner utterly, fully, actively. Their bodies rode each other like tidal waves, accumulating pleasure and releasing it in the form of Elle's increasingly louder moans.

When Maya tipped her over the edge, she felt as if taken by a waterfall, flowing down with the water, dangerously accelerating but still within the flow of herself. Their foreheads met, and they experienced a sweet, deserved tiredness.

"Should we shower?" Maya said, resting against Elle's torso.

"We should."

Showering was another problem that Elle had encountered after her injury. Now in her bathroom there were three stools at all times, supporting her in every activity that would otherwise require standing. She had to shower sitting down and felt quite peculiar about it.

With Maya everything felt easy, however.

In the shower, they joked around, helping each other wash their backs, enjoying the cool stream of water falling down on their smiling faces. Elle couldn't believe her luck to be with the person she loved freely and joyfully. She wanted to contain every single moment in her memory, replay it before falling asleep every night. With Maya she could forget about her injury, she could forget about the anxiety of not getting back to her job. All that mattered was that they stood (and sat) together under the shower, joking and spilling lavender-scented soap everywhere.

"We should probably get out. We're wasting so much water," Maya noticed, looking at Elle. Her eyes were sparkling beautifully.

"Wherever you go, I go," Elle sang very badly, but it was okay. Neither of them could sing very well. "You'll need to help me up, though," she added casually.

Brushing their teeth, they looked at each other in the mirror reflection. Elle didn't know how it could be possible to find someone who looked so impossibly beautiful when she was simply brushing her teeth, naked except for an old t-shirt. She preferred this version of Maya out of all of them. She loved it when Maya would get dressed up with her tasteful makeup and elaborate hair, but she knew that there was no other way for her to be more beautiful than simply standing naked after the shower, brushing her teeth. Nothing could beat that simple, intimate beauty accessible only to Elle.

"I'll miss you at work," Maya said, having spat out the toothpaste. "Can't wait to live with you."

"You'll still have to work when we live together. You know that, right?" Elle laughed. "Unless we want to retire early and sit in our beautiful garden all day growing tomatoes and listening to classical music."

"Hmm…" Maya looked at Elle with a carefree smile. "Fifteen more years and we have a deal. We'll grow tomatoes and listen to classical music in our lovely garden. Should we grow cucumbers, as well?"

"I don't know how cucumbers grow," Elle admitted, "but I can learn."

They went back to the bedroom, Elle with Maya's support. She was getting used to accepting

Maya's help without being weird about it, realizing it was only temporary, understanding that she'd be ready to do the same for her. The ceiling window looked out on the night sky, starless due to the city's light pollution.

"Isn't it sad," Maya dived into an embrace with Elle, their bodies keeping each other warm in the pleasant air chilled by night, the windows in the room were left slightly open, "That we can't see any stars from here? I love Phoenix Ridge, but sometimes I wish I lived somewhere far from the city, somewhere remote where the sky is still beautiful."

'It is slightly upsetting," Elle agreed, adding, "But don't you think it's beautiful in its own way, the fact that we've built our own stars and they eclipsed the sky? We're living among them now." She smiled at the thought. "We're our own little blinking stars."

"That's a nice way to put it." Elle felt Maya nod against her chest. It was so pleasant to feel each other so close that they didn't have to look for each other's reactions, only feel them against their skin.

"I have a question," Maya said after a while. "Did you have dreams during your coma? I never asked, but I thought about it quite a lot."

Elle took some time to think. "I did," she answered. "They mostly consisted of remote memories floating around blurring into each other. It was a strange experience, though very peaceful. I could feel myself floating around my mind, never in control, simply carried by its currents."

"Do you remember anything specific?" Maya prompted.

"I remember one memory of the sea. It was very peaceful. I'd completely forgotten about it until then. When I was a little child, my family and I used to camp on the beach for many days during the summer. When I was six or seven, I started sneaking out of the tent to walk along the beach in the early morning when my parents were still asleep." Elle ran her fingers through Maya's still wet hair, wishing they could visit the sea themselves.

"That sounds beautiful," Maya said dreamily. "We rarely know what happens to patients during a coma. It's still a bit of a mystery. Some wake up saying they don't remember being in any state of dreaming, while some wake up saying they had nightmares in repeat. I'm glad that for you it was rather calm. The way you describe it sounds pensive."

"It was, in a way. I felt completely alone with myself. In a good way." Elle fixed the sheets around them. "I also dreamed of our fight, the one that ended our relationship before."

"Oh, I'm sorry." Maya looked up to find Elle's eyes. "How did it make you feel?"

"I think I understood your emotions better than ever. In the dreams, I didn't fully remember people. I don't think I knew your name when the scene was replaying in my mind, but I was very attuned to the feelings floating around the room. It prompted me to form a proper apology to you."

For a while they remained quiet, not knowing what to say. Maya's thumb traced along Elle's arm, and Elle enjoyed the slightly tickling sensation.

"I'm glad it brought us closer in the end," Maya finally said, yawning a little. "I'm grateful for whatever has led us here. I wouldn't change anything. Besides your injury, of course," she added quickly.

"Fuck my injury. I'll get out of it." Elle kissed Maya's head. "I'm glad to have you here. It's the perfect place for you to be, I think."

"I agree," Maya said, yawning again, and Elle could feel her drifting off to sleep.

Soon, she felt her chest rise and fall in the steady rhythm of sleep. Elle didn't want to follow, afraid of losing the sensation of Maya asleep against her body, wrapped up in her duvet. She embraced her, looking up to see the starless night sky through her window. From time to time she watched an airplane pass. She knew that her house was on some flying route, the airport being south of the city. She didn't feel sleepy at all, instead soaking in the intimate night, bathing in the calm atmosphere. She tried matching her breath to Maya's, holding it in after each inhale to even it out.

She felt good as a quiet observer, watching the clouds roll about the sky, listening in to the peaceful silence. Breath in, breath out, she tried keeping up with Maya's sleepful rhythm. When she finally succeeded, the sky was becoming more purple with each new drop of sunlight, and her eyes closed with the first signs of dawn.

"Get up, Darling, the sun is shining and I'll have to go soon," Maya sang to Elle, touching her shoulder.

"Hi." Elle sat up, slightly disoriented. "I thought you'd be gone by now. You said you had an early shift today?" She looked at the clock, which read clearly 8:20 a.m.

"I'm a liar though." Maya laughed. "I start later. I'll be working through the night. I made you breakfast, can you smell it?"

"Are you kidding me?" Elle inhaled a faint scent of something floury and sugary rising from downstairs. "I love you, but what the hell."

She delighted in the way the words *I love you* could comfortably roll from her tongue now, so fitting and effortless. She put on some clothes that came flying to her from the top of the drawer, then let Maya help her descend the stairs.

"What'd you make?" she inquired, impatient.

"Crepes. You had all the ingredients, so I thought *why not.*" She kissed Elle's forehead. "Bon Appetit. We need to eat them fast. I still need to go by my house before work."

They sat down and began assembling their crepes, honey and chestnut spread, fig jam and cottage cheese. The sweet smell decorated the entire kitchen, and Elle couldn't believe this was now her life. The warm crepe almost dissolved in her mouth.

"You're a master crepe maker," she mumbled around a mouthful of food.

"Don't exaggerate." Maya waved her hand. "You deserved it after yesterday's masterful dinner."

Maya finished eating and collected the plates, then began gathering up her things. They both knew she wouldn't get all of them, and it wouldn't matter, because she'd be back in no time. This comfort relaxed them both.

With the corners of her lips still full of jam, she laid a sticky kiss on Elle's cheek.

"I need to get going. I had a lovely time with you."

"Wait a second." Elle removed the jam with her finger. "There you go, *doctor*."

"Very funny." Maya rolled her eyes. "I'll be back with you in no time, you know that?"

"I know." Elle nodded.

"Now don't get cocky." Maya kissed Elle's lips tenderly. They got stuck in an embrace for a moment, then pulled away.

"I really need to go." She picked up her back and put on the autumn coat. At the door, she turned to add, "I love you!"

"I love you too," Elle responded before the door closed.

EPILOGUE
4 YEARS LATER

"Maybe Teresa?" Maya shouted toward the kitchen from where sounds of vacuuming reached her ears. The spring cleaning was in full bloom.

Elle's head appeared next to the door frame. She furrowed her eyebrows. "Teresa? Like Mother Teresa? Are you joking?"

Maya laughed. "Don't make fun of me. I thought it'd be cute."

"And the nickname would be Tess? No, I don't like it." Having stated her opinion, Elle got back to vacuuming.

Ever since Maya had entered her third trimester, Elle had to take care of every chore around the house, and she did so with pleasure.

Sometimes tired pleasure, but pleasure regardless. She made it her goal to have the house as clean as possible for spring. Spring and the end of Maya's pregnancy, of course. *We'll have a little spring baby,* she'd think, often getting excited over the prospect.

"Anna?" She heard from the living room.

"No! Too basic," she shouted, shaking her head. None of the names felt *right*. None of them sounded well enough in her ears. The debate had been going on for weeks.

"In a second I'll give up and leave you alone with it," Maya threatened from her place in the living room. She was joking, but there was a note of genuine irritation in her voice.

Elle turned off the vacuum cleaner and walked out of the kitchen. She was ready to get it done, to choose the perfect name. It was March, and the sun would make everything easier, or so she believed. Nothing could be unbeatable during spring. Its lightness of being made everything equally light and sweet, fresh like the flowers decorating their windows.

"All right, let's do it." She sat next to Maya, automatically laying her hand gently on Maya's bulging belly. Sometimes she'd feel legs furiously kicking, and she couldn't contain her pride. "What are our top choices, hmm?"

Maya had waited for this moment the entire day. She felt that Elle didn't understand how overwhelming it was to choose something that would become an integral part of their daughter's life, arguably an integral part of their daughter.

"You didn't *approve* of many I suggested," she looked at Elle accusingly. "How about you think of some?" To soften the accusation, she laid a kiss on Elle's cheek, giving her the piece of paper with noted down names.

"Hm..." Elle furrowed her eyebrows, scanning the list and thinking of potential additions.

She didn't want to admit this to Maya, but the perspective of naming the baby filled her with a quiet kind of terror. Naming her meant putting the last piece together before birth, making it more real than anything before. With a name, she would finally become a person.

Going through the names often caused her to think of her ancestors, and of Maya's ancestors, too, of everyone who'd come before them. The legacy they'd be passing on, something ancient and tender, alive. She tried remembering the names of her ancestors as far back as she could, straining her mind to reach the names of people separated from her by hundreds of years. At first, she thought it would be an honorable thing to name her daughter something traditional and tie her to Elle's family history. But what about Maya's ancestors, and why would they decide to weigh the baby down with the chain of the past?

"What are we looking for in the name?" She turned to look at Maya. "What do you want it to be like?"

"That's a good question." Maya nodded. "I guess I hadn't thought of it that way. Let me think." She took Elle's hand while pausing to ponder the question. Their fingers interlaced, a little witness to their habitual intimacy. Noticing these habits never failed to make Maya smile. "I want her not to feel limited by the name, first of all. You know these names like Rose, or Daisy? They're so beautiful, but I think they assume the girl to come to be sweet and feminine like the flowers. I want our daughter to feel free to express herself however she likes without her name constraining her in any way."

Elle smiled. "That's considerate of you. What else?"

"I don't want it to have a silly nickname

attached, like Tessy." She laughed. "Though I still think Teresa is a lovely name. How about you? Do you have anything you'd like the name to be or avoid being?"

Maya looked so focused and so beautiful that Elle couldn't find an answer in her head besides to lean in and kiss her. The fresh fragrance of her hair tickled Elle's nose, and she couldn't imagine a better afternoon than sitting on their own couch and considering what to name their soon to arrive daughter. Maya gently pulled away, shaking her head.

"Stop distracting us," she reprimanded. "You're too sweet. We need to get this done. We'll still need to get used to the name."

"Oh, I think we'll have plenty of time for that." Elle smiled. "How am I supposed to stay focused when my beautiful girlfriend is sitting right next to me, and her lips taste the best they ever have?"

Maya laughed. "Elle, you say that every time we kiss."

"Every time you taste better." Elle winked. "The names. All right. I've been thinking about tradition a lot, ever since you got pregnant. To what degree should we honor our ancestors, in what ways, and all that. About the identity of our daughter. I think the name ties into that."

"So what, do you want to choose some name of one of our ancestors?" Maya asked.

"See, I was thinking about that. But then, I don't think it would really fit who we are as a couple, would it? And who's going to be more important to our daughter than her moms? So let's choose something fresh that will reflect us as people."

"Also, our ancestors were probably homophobic." Maya laughed.

"Or maybe some of them were closeted and forced to hide their whole life," Elle pondered, "and now we honor their life by openly celebrating who we are? I prefer to think of it that way. And those who were straight and homophobic, they'd probably change their minds if they saw us now."

"You're so distracted today, really." Maya kissed Elle's forehead. "Back to the names. What do you think about Alex?"

"Alex?"

"Mhmm." Maya nodded. "It's universal, short and cute, could be feminine or masculine, and I think it matches our names." After a moment, she added, "And surnames."

"I like it, Alex Monroe-Rodriguez." Elle took Maya in her arms, excited. "I think we've got it! Alex Monroe-Rodriguez, with such a long double surname, a short name works perfectly. I love you." She rocked Maya in her arms side to side, unable to let her go.

The world outside looked bright and saturated, the grass around the house glistening under the plentiful sun, its green leaves vibrant and inviting, carrying shadows of the passing clouds here and there. It was a lovely March day.

"So, is it decided? Her name is Alex?" Maya freed herself from the tight embrace to look at Elle's face. She couldn't wait to see Elle as a mom.

"It's decided." Elle nodded, happiness sparkling in her eyes. "Should we begin preparing for the dinner party?"

"Yes!" Maya got up excitedly, and a wave of nausea overcame her. She couldn't wait to meet her daughter, but she also needed this pregnancy to come to an end for more selfish reasons. "Next time you're the one getting pregnant," she threatened.

Elle looked petrified. "Not in a million years, Baby, I'm not as tough as you are."

"Sure." Maya sighed. She didn't feel particularly tough, only nauseated and heavy.

They entered the freshly cleaned kitchen. Its large window let in a flood of sunlight, which then shone on the surface of light wood countertops and the stone floor. Maya gasped.

"You really outdid yourself, Elle," she said while kissing her neck and reaching to open the fridge. "What were we supposed to make?"

"Ginger garlic chicken with broccoli and sesame chili sauce as the main, cucumber and onion dip with vegetables as the appetizer, lavender martinis as the drink," she recited military style.

Maya looked at her lovingly with a little smile. "Who'd think you'd become such a house chef?" She reached to kiss her, and they locked in a long, sensual one, full of love and hope for the days to come.

"Will you let me cook now?" Elle said in a serious tone of voice, making Maya laugh. "You can stay in the kitchen, though. If you want. I'll bring you a chair."

And she was gone to fetch a chair from the living room. The hours spent together in the kitchen had quickly become one of their favorite ways to spend time, usually with Elle doing everything and delegating small tasks like peeling vegetables to Maya. It made them feel like a proper family to sit in their own kitchen and prepare food together, and they couldn't wait until their baby would join them in the ritual. Elle came back in carrying the chair.

"Let's get this started," she said, opening the fridge in a grand motion. "The bird has been waiting for us in the fridge. You can mix the sauce, Maya."

They cooked and jived to light jazz music, the fragrance of roasted chicken spread in the air and infected them both with powerful hunger. Maya bravely mixed all the sauces and dips, feeling helpful and a part of the cooking. Elle enjoyed flexing her skills when she explained to Maya the process of preparing the chicken.

"Elle, this is disgusting, I don't want to listen to that," Maya complained, twisting her face away.

"No but you don't understand. It's so satisfying, I'll show you how to do it next time," Elle teased, knowing fully well that Maya was disgusted by the process of preparing meat. She still ate it—she just preferred not to know how exactly the thing got to be on her plate.

"Shouldn't you set up the table outside? We don't have that much time."

"Right. Right." And Elle was out of the kitchen.

Their garden was perfect for dinner parties, and they took advantage of it as often as they could. When they'd found the property, only twenty minutes away from the city, they'd fallen in love with it at once. Its garden spread wide, full of cherry trees and flower bushes, a little bit wild in its beauty. Elle wanted to dig a pond somewhere in it, but she'd never gotten around doing it, so after a while, everyone would get annoyed whenever she'd start talking about it.

Whenever the weather allowed, they'd set up a long table there for the guests and delighted in the knowledge that they were the best hosting couple among their friends.

"What tablecloth do we want, Darling?" Elle shouted from the garden. Sometimes she'd catch herself saying things like this and giggle at their domesticity, sounding like the married couples she'd see on TV as a child. Now she was one of them, and she wouldn't change a thing about it.

"The Italian one?"

"Excuse me, which one is the Italian one?"

"The blue checkered one!" Maya looked out

the window. "Do you remember? The Italian guy gave it to us that summer."

"Oh... I know which one," Elle lied. "Can you check on the chicken? It should be ready."

If she could, she'd host dinner parties every weekend. There seemed something so graceful about welcoming friends into their home and the organizational zeal that preceded the party.

She knew that once Alex would be born things would change. Their energy wouldn't allow for these as often. But there'd be other exciting things to come.

"Elle, should it look like this?" Maya's concerned voice reached her out of the kitchen.

"Like what?!" Elle's blood ran cold. She ran to the kitchen at once. "DID YOU BURN MY CHICKEN?"

The bird sat on its plate covered in coal black. Elle sat down on the kitchen chair, lamenting.

"Oh no, I'm so sorry Baby. I didn't know I had to hurry with it..." Maya touched Elle's back.

"It's fine," Elle said unconvincingly. "It's fine. We can scrape the burned parts off a little. I'm sure it'll still be good inside. It's fine."

"I'll set the table, all right?" Maya said, wanting

to leave Elle to her own devices in trying to fix the chicken.

Setting the table was one of the favorite parts for Maya. She'd grown in her mastery of decorations, setting the table with flowers, and buying beautiful cutlery. She felt as if she was in a fairytale, having grown up in a house that couldn't afford anything of the sort, especially not a garden. She put blue-tinted flowers into empty wine bottles, making the sturdy table as beautiful as it could be. Then she made space for candles, going back into the house to fetch them.

"How's the chicken looking?" She laid her hand on Elle's back, wanting to be as supportive as she could.

"Not terrible." Elle grunted like a sculptor in the middle of a creative flow. "I'm fixing it."

Maya nodded, not wanting to interrupt, and went to look for the candles. She had a clear aesthetic vision for the evening, she wanted it all to be full of flowers and warm candlelight, the perfect background for lovely conversations. The heaps of unnecessary trinkets in the drawers of their house always brought a smile to Maya's face. They were little insignificant witnesses to her life together with Elle.

"Maya, they'll be here in twenty minutes!"

"I'm almost ready!"

The light outside took on a more evening tint, the clouds bathing in light orange and pink of the approaching sunset. The temperature dropped a little, making the perspective of a warm meal even more delicious. The first guests began showing up, handing Maya and Elle bottles of wine and kissing their cheeks.

"I brought you something great." Fleur flashed her teeth in a darling smile, "It's the best non-alcoholic wine I've ever tasted." She gave Maya the bottle and the two shared a long embrace.

"It's so good to see you again." Maya finally let her go. "Thank you so much for the wine. We will definitely taste it tonight!"

Soon, the firefighters flooded the little garden gate, some accompanied by their partners. Elle hugged everyone tightly, making light conversation and slowly leading them toward the table. She put on instrumental music, uncorked the abundant wine, and finally commanded everyone to take a seat because she and Maya had been starving for a while already and couldn't wait anymore for the food. The group giggled, admitting they'd also had been waiting to taste Elle's impeccable cuisine. She nodded gratefully, then went inside to retrieve the dishes.

"Do you need any help?" Maya turned around, looking in Elle's direction.

"No, no, sit down, I'll manage," Elle responded, hurrying to get everything.

"She gets so despotic in the kitchen." Maya laughed with her friends once Elle was gone from their sight.

Elle soon emerged out of the kitchen with the appetizers, platters of vegetables and bowls with dips. Everyone dug into them as soon as she set them on the table. No conversation could survive the competition with food. The sounds of biting down and chewing filled everyone's ears, and soon most of the vegetables were gone. The simmering of conversations resumed, slowly building up to the wonderful noise of excited speech.

"Have you thought of a name yet?" O'Malley asked.

"Yes, actually, we decided today." Maya looked lovingly at Elle, taking her hand. "She's going to be named Alex."

The gathering began clapping their hands. "What a nice name. Congratulations!"

Overcome with excitement, Maya had to feel

Elle's lips on her own. They locked in a long kiss, forgetting those around them.

"All right, all right, guys. Don't be so disgustingly sweet." Haley rolled her eyes.

"Haley, leave them be. They're wonderful." Kaia smiled, leaning on Hallie.

Elle pulled away from the kiss. "I should get the chicken. It should be warmed up already." he sgot up and ran into the kitchen again.

"I'll go help her." Kaia got up as well and followed Elle into the house.

The rest of the company sipped on their wine, enjoying the last rays of the evening sun. Maya sat quietly observing her friends for a while, delighting in the sight of them all sitting in her garden enjoying Elle's cooking and each other's company. She didn't even have to participate in the conversation to feel its warmth, to feel included. She knew she could join in any time, and they'd welcome her gladly.

"Maya, what do you think of the new department director?" Fleur turned to her.

"Who, the young guy?" Maya studied Fleur's face, sensing something interesting. "I don't know, I think it was a strange choice to make him the director, but I suppose he's charismatic."

"Fleur likes him," Haley said from her corner of the table. "A lot."

"Oh?" Maya laughed. "Really?"

Everyone's attention turned to them, hungry for light-hearted gossip.

"Well," Fleur got flustered, "as long as it wouldn't be unprofessional…"

"I mean," Hallie raised her eyebrows, "I'm not the one to judge, but I think you're fine."

And with that, the chicken finally arrived, carried by Kaia. Behind her walked Elle, carrying the sides. Salads and fingerling potatoes. Everything was beautifully fragrant, filling the air with a promise of nourishing food. The little *ah's* and *oh's* of approval were honey to the hosts' ears.

"You two are spoiling us." O'Malley shook her head,.

"Only the best for the best." Maya winked at her, more than ready to dive into the food.

The chicken was quickly divided, and Elle watched in awe as everyone devoured her food. Soon, the platters stood empty and the little plates were busy with forks and knives dancing around, from time to time screeching, causing the guests to giggle here and there.

"Elle, this is magnificent," Hallie raised her head from her plate, her eyes wide in wonder.

"Thanks. It's quite a simple recipe," Elle said humbly, even though she didn't feel humble at all. She felt proud and satisfied to be able to be able to feed her friends so well, and in some corner of her heart, she knew that she'd make her mother proud, too.

When the knives and forks had finally been laid down, the time for serious and deep conversations began, as with most dinner parties. When the minds were relaxed by the wine, or in other cases the social atmosphere of openness and love, the topics one wishes to only discuss with close friends began to emerge. Everyone sat back in their chairs, taking in the sweet air of the late spring evening.

"I've been meaning to ask for so long," Hallie said to Elle, and everyone listened in. "When are you planning to go back to full service at the station? We miss you." She looked around for confirmation in the other firefighters' faces.

"Yeah, she's right. We've been asking this ourselves a lot," Haley added.

Elle smiled, always honored to be in the thoughts of her friends, knowing she couldn't avoid the subject for long anymore. She reached for Maya's hand under the table. They'd been discussing this with each other for a long time, and now the moment had finally come to tell their friends.

"I'm not going to be back at the station," Elle said in a serious tone. "I'll take care of talent management part time. I would like to spend time raising our daughter now, especially because Maya's job is already so demanding."

The news created a large stir around the table, their friends looked at each other surprised. Elle knew the decision would be controversial, but she felt good about it and wouldn't have any problems explaining her point of view. Maya tightened her grasp on Elle's hand, wanting to show her support.

"Are you sure?" Hallie asked, raising her eyebrows "You're a great firefighter, and having fully recovered, too... We could use your skills, and you can work only two days a week, anyway."

"I'm sure. I want to commit my time to Alex, and because of the injury and me not working there for a long time anyway, it doesn't feel like a big loss. I'll still be friends with you, just as we are now, but I feel that a new chapter of my life is opening, and I want to welcome it accordingly."

"I think that's a very responsible decision." Fleur nodded, smiling at Elle. "I'm sure you'll be a great mom."

"Thank you, Fleur." Elle smiled at her in response. Being told she'd make a great mother stirred something tender deep inside of her. It was an intense compliment for her to receive.

"I don't know." Hallie looked unconvinced. "You can be a great parent and not sacrifice your career. And don't you want your daughter to grow up with this message?"

Elle took the time to ponder the question. "I think she'll see that when it comes to Maya. But I also want her to know that it's okay to make family life a priority. These things are equally important. Besides, it's not a question of me leaving – rather reentering. Perhaps it's a sign that my time as an active firefighter was meant to end."

"I'd have never expected that." O'Malley shook her head, "Definitely not from you. But if that's what you feel is the next step for you, then I wish you good luck and will always be there to support you two." She looked at Elle then Maya, smiling.

"People change." Elle turned to face Maya and winked. "They really do."

"Well, just don't let Maya overwork herself,

hmm?" Fleur added, reaching out to touch Maya's shoulder.

"Oh, we'll make sure she doesn't," Elle said. "We've been thinking of going on a long trip once our baby is past her first birthday."

They plunged into discussions of travel and preferred destinations and everyone's favorite airlines. Advice for travelling with little children was being tossed around, even though no one actually had had a child yet. The atmosphere was mellow, and wanting to end the evening on a lovely note, Elle got up with a suggestion.

"Should we do a little dance party and annoy our already very annoyed neighbors?"

Everyone approved of the idea, pushing the table aside and making space to dance. Elle chose her favorite jazzy songs and some vintage hits like Presley. Everyone got to slow dance in a couple or twirl around the dance floor, free and careless, as if they didn't have to work tomorrow, as if they wouldn't need to leave the garden at some point, the heavenly garden without any forbidden fruits. Maya swayed from side to side, feeling a little too tired to dance, and Elle quickly joined her to keep her company, swaying together with her.

The scents of the garden came blooming stronger with each new day, flowers and trees spreading their fragrances all around the house. Living so close to a small fragment of nature filled both Maya and Elle with an inexplicable sense of joy. Having grown up in a big city in apartments with no gardens or even balcony, their only experiences of it consisted of parks. But this little garden of their own, beautiful and peaceful, shaded with trees and full of bushes, was a place so different from the crowded parks that they considered it much more valuable than their house. They couldn't wait to bring up a child in such an endearing place.

The hour was getting late, and even though everyone was filled with a dance-induced charm and didn't want to leave the hosts in peace, they forced upon themselves to the realization that sooner or later, the wonderful time would have to end. One by one, car by car, they began to leave, promising to visit as soon as an opportunity would show itself.

"Take care of each other." Fleur hugged them both, tender and kind as always.

Her steps sounded gracefully on the stone pavement before the gate shut behind her. The last guests left were Hallie and Kaia, who came up to say goodbye while holding hands.

"I still will need time to get used to the idea of you permanently going away from our team, I wasn't expecting that at all, but here we are... I always thought you'd return after your injury was healed." Hallie looked at Elle for a long time, then shifted her gaze towards Maya. "But I know what a miracle it is to be deeply in love, so deeply that one learns to make sacrifices and changes that seem drastic to the outside world. I hope you'll stay as happy as you seem to be right now." she smiled, squeezing Kaia's hand.

"I wish you the same," Kaia added. "And whether or not Elle comes back won't change anything about our friendship. If anything, you'll just have to organize more dinner parties. Or we will!" She looked at Hallie, and they both laughed, because neither of them felt particularly passionate about cooking.

"Yes, we'll hire Elle as the cook, though," Hallie added. "It would be better for everyone involved."

"Sorry, guys. I'm only one household's private

chef." Elle shook her head, "I'm afraid I'm taken." She pulled Maya closer and kissed her forehead.

"Take care, girls." Hallie and Kaia came up to embrace them and then turned to follow everyone else through the gate, giggling and joking to each other.

Elle and Maya stood following the guests out with their eyes, taking in the beautiful sight of satiated, laughing friends leaving their garden with promises of return on their smiling lips. They looked up to see the stars, although still dimmed, much more visible than in the heart of the city.

"Remember when we were looking at the sky at your old house, and the stars just weren't there?" Maya stroked Elle's back up and down, the gentle massage she knew Elle loved.

"That was one of the luckiest nights of my life," Elle said, smiling. "I understood then that you really meant to stay, and we'd truly be together again for good."

"Did you not believe me before?" Maya laughed. "That's rude."

"I believed you. I didn't know whether to believe myself... Whether I wouldn't mess it up down the line or get scared. But that night I understood I wouldn't allow anything of the sort to happen, and you were there, loving and kind and everything I had ever wanted my love to be."

"Don't be so sweet." Maya climbed up her toes to kiss Elle's cheek, something that required significant effort at this stage of pregnancy. "We need to clean up the mess now."

Elle sighed, "we do, don't we?" She looked at Maya. "You know what? I'll clean it up. You go and take a bath and relax. I'll be done in no time."

"More like you'll be done at 5 a.m." Maya looked at her watch poignantly.

"Then I'll finish the rest tomorrow morning."

She kissed Maya's lips, wishing to linger on them more, but promising herself to commit to the cleaning and finish it swiftly.

"Well, I won't protest," Maya said, turning to go back into the house.

The dishes were stacked on the crowded table, the candles were half-burned through stood cluttering the surface, and the tablecloth was stained with sauces. Elle sighed. Everyone loved to come and eat, but not many stayed to help them clean. She smiled to herself wearily. If they kept having these gatherings this often, the guests will have to start participating in the cleaning rituals, as well. She felt strangely at peace collecting the dishes and carrying them to the kitchen, gradually seeing the table cleaned off and the dishwasher working.

Until she heard Maya shouting.

"Elle! ELLE!" Her voice thundered downstairs.

"What happened?" Elle ran up, terrified by the anxiety in Maya's voice. "What--"

"My water broke," Maya said, standing in the bathroom and looking shocked.

"Fuck." Elle felt her chest tighten with stress, pulsing in her temples. "We should go to the hospital, right?"

"Yes." Maya nodded. "Yes. Let's go."

Elle's thoughts were running at the speed of light and were tangling themselves as a result. They got into the car and sped to Maya's hospital where she knew the midwives and felt the most comfortable.

"I was hoping labor would start with peaceful contractions and I'd be able to stay home," Maya said from the back seat.

"That's fine. It's fine," Elle kept repeating. "Everything will be all right. It doesn't matter how labor started, only that it will end well." She glanced at Maya in the rearview mirror.

"Are you reassuring me or yourself?" Maya

laughed weakly, feeling the contractions growing in strength.

"Are you all right?" Elle glanced back again.

"I'm in labor, Elle." Maya knit her eyebrows together. "Keep your eyes on the road, okay?"

"Sure. Sure." Elle gripped the wheel tighter.

In her entire career as a firefighters' driver, she'd never experienced the amount of stress soaring through her veins as she did now while driving through the night streets to the hospital with Maya. The shapes of street lamps and passing cars seemed blurred in her determination to get there fast, the focus on speed taking her thoughts away from the anxiety of Maya giving birth. As a firefighter, she witnessed a few emergency births, but nothing could have prepared her for experiencing her love at the beginning of labor, the journey she knew would be painful and tiring.

"How are you doing?" she asked again, this time still keeping her eyes on the road.

"The same as before." Maya's voice reached Elle's ears. "Fucking stressed, too."

As a doctor, Maya knew exactly what was happening and would happen with her body, yet the experience itself was similar to nothing she had experienced before. The feeling of her body putting all its efforts into one place, one horribly difficult action pulsed through her mind, and she was so, so glad to be with Elle in this moment. She wouldn't want anyone else in the world to be with her in the delivery room.

Upon getting to the hospital, Elle realized she'd have to pull herself together and offer her calm support the way she'd done in the past. The nurses led them to a delivery room through a series of artificial smelling corridors, white walls licked by LED lights. Elle knew Maya would be in the best hands, yet still she couldn't help feeling that this was the highest stakes situation of her life, with two people she cared about the most directly concerned—her love and her child. Her heartbeat nested in her throat, and as she entered the birthing room, cold sweat began running down her back.

"You'll be all right." She took Maya's hand in her own. "I'll be here the whole time."

"Are you sure *you're* all right?" Maya looked at Elle in concern. "You look like a ghost."

"Dear, I'm about to pass out from stress, but it's not about me today." Elle showed her thumbs up, as she couldn't think of anything more to say. She desperately wanted to be able to talk to Maya and tell her important things, valuable advice or some encouraging words, but her mind was like a lightning bolt, immediate and overcome with sensations, electrifying and quite useless.

For the entire labor, Maya was free to move around, and she did, feeling very restless. They joked with Elle that the baby would be sporty, forcing her mother to participate in her hyperactive ways. Maya couldn't be more grateful for the little jokes. Whenever Elle would say some lighthearted comment she felt secure.

When the contractions got the most intense, however, Maya lay down. For some time, Elle thought she couldn't stand being in the room anymore, but she couldn't be out of it, either. She generally felt as if her existence was in an in-between state that could end only together with the birth, her state of being hanging by the thinnest of threads.

She held Maya's hand. Maya gripped Elle so tightly that the blood stopped flowing to her fingers, and then when she no longer wanted it, Elle began pacing the room like mad, circling around and occasionally bumping into the irritated-with-her midwife.

The midwife kept saying that Maya was indeed

doing great, and no complications were on the way, but Elle's thoughts were stubborn, or perhaps it was more her heart, because her thoughts themselves seemed to soar off somewhere inaccessible, leaving her only with love and anxiety racing through her mind.

Push, push, that the midwife had been repeating for a long time burned into her skull, only *push,* and Maya's face twisted with pain, groans that sounded like death, but she knew they in fact meant only life—hopefully meant only life. Definitely meant only life. That was what the midwife kept saying.

"How is she doing?" she asked a nurse, her face as white as a sheet and glistening with beads of sweat, her hair stuck to her temples.

"She's doing great, darling. There really isn't much to worry about." The nurse patted Elle's back. "You look like you're the one giving birth."

Their exchange was interrupted by an enthusiastic shout.

"Look, the head!" The midwife pointed it out with her finger for Maya to see, but Maya was too tired to look. She only sighed with relief. "Is she alive?" The question had been beating around her mind the entire time. The only thing she felt besides the struggle and pain was the anxiety. *Is she alive?*

"Of course she's alive!" The midwife seemed almost angry at such a silly question. "Of course she is. I'd have told you otherwise. Now push, push, stay strong."

While everyone was busy, dawn slowly crept up the delivery room's windows. Amidst the gentle strokes of early light, the sound everyone had been waiting for filled the room with screaming new life. The little girl was crying, and together with her, Maya and Elle. When the umbilical cord had been cut and the baby dried off with a towel, she rested on Maya's chest, calming down and quietly breathing, making little sounds that melted everyone's hearts. Elle embraced Maya, kissing her sweaty face and trying desperately not to cry but then realizing that this would probably be the best moment to do so.

"Can I hold her?" she asked, gently stroking the little girl's hair.

"Of course." Maya delicately passed the towel-wrapped baby into Elle's arms. "She's perfect" Maya declared, looking at her child lovingly, then meeting Elle's eyes.

"She absolutely is." Elle nodded, kissing the

newborn's head. Nothing existed to her in that moment besides her daughter and Maya. "Hello, Alex, nice to meet you."

Silver paths of tears decorated both their faces, happy and exhausted. It felt only right that their daughter saw the world at dawn, welcomed by a newborn sun embacing the clouds with a soft, pink glow. The occasional flock of birds graced the sky, and the streets were empty, with only bakers working on their morning bread. The couple looked outside the window at the peaceful scenery, holding their baby and each other's hands, wondering how on Earth their lives could contain so much beauty.

WHAT'S NEXT?

Thank you so much for reading! I hope you loved Maya and Elle's story as much as I loved writing them.

Please do check out the next book in the Phoenix Ridge Fire series Flame Kissed.

Firefighter Leilani Silva saves the life of a billionaire CEO and there is a burning attraction between them. They live in different worlds. Can they find a way past their differences and is the connection they have more than just a spark?

What's next?

mybook.to/PRF3

FREE BOOK

I really hope you enjoyed this story. I loved writing it.

I'd love for you to get my FREE book- Her Boss- by joining my mailing list. On my mailing list you can be the first to find out about free or discounted books or new releases and get short sexy stories for free! Just click on the following link or type into your web browser: https://BookHip.com/MNVVPBP

Meg has had a huge crush on her hot older boss for

some time now. Could it be possible that her crush is reciprocated? https://BookHip.com/MNVVPBP

Printed in Great Britain
by Amazon